ESCAPE FROM THE FRONT

ERWIN. (ERV) KRAUSE

authorHOUSE

AuthorHouse™
1663 Liberty Drive
Bloomington, IN 47403
www.authorhouse.com
Phone: 833-262-8899

Published by AuthorHouse 01/29/2021

ISBN: 978-1-6655-1420-0 (sc)
ISBN: 978-1-6655-1418-7 (hc)
ISBN: 978-1-6655-1419-4 (e)

Library of Congress Control Number: 2021901208

Print information available on the last page.

In Praise of Those Who Pick up Hitchhikers

I did a lot of hitchhiking in my younger days. Some of these rides were solicited out of necessity having to do with a frequently limited budget. At other times, circumstances permitted this mode of travel as my only option. And to be honest, there were times I hitched for a taste of adventure.

Some experiences were memorable. While hitching in Montana, I was once given a ride by a man from a nearby Hutterite colony. The bearded elder came along after I had already spent hours of desperation watching scores of suspicious motorists pass me by. For the next hour, he and I enjoyed a most enriching conversation (for me, at least) in the cab of his pickup. Though I have since forgotten his name, I will never forget him as a person. He became part of the inspiration for this story.

I know that most folks don't pick up hitchhikers these days. But some still do. They are the ones who still acknowledge the Esperanto of the extended thumb. The ones who apply the brakes and dare to invite a perfect stranger into their car. Only a select few realize that by this simple act of kindness, they are participating in an age-old rite of mutual trust— something we need now more than ever.

CONTENTS

ACKNOWLEDGMENTS

After dozens of revisions on my own, I handed the manuscript over to Judi Turkheimer of KENDALL Park, New Jersey. Her skillful tweaking resulted in a far more readable story while allowing me to maintain my own voice.

I would like also to thank Cleo Carrigan and the creative team at AuthorHouse for their professional guidance during the final publishing stage.

For the past two years, I have participated in a writing workshop led by Chris Palermo at the Oakdale Public Library on Long Island. The camaraderie and support of these fine people has meant more to me than they realize.

I reserve a special debt of gratitude for the ongoing encouragement of my friends and family, but especially my partner and collaborator-in-life, Lois Hoffman. If she ever had doubts about my zany story, she was kind enough to keep them to herself.

CHAPTER 1

THE SCREAM

You would have heard if you were anywhere in the vicinity of 42 Harbor Hill Way, Sea Cliff, Long Island on the afternoon of the summer solstice a few years ago: a full-throated wail. It came from a modest, white cedar clapboard colonial with a decibel level that easily penetrated its sturdy plaster walls. Comic book fans may have seen a huge word bubble Aaaaaaargh!!! suspended in the air a few agonizing seconds before scattering in the breeze. For art connoisseurs, the moment would have evoked Edvard Munch's iconic painting, "The Scream". Those who subscribe to the "If You See (Hear?) Something, Say Something!" imperative would have promptly dialed 911.

Only a few minutes earlier, Will Kraft had returned home from his teaching job. No one was there, as he had anticipated, since his wife, Katie, had earlier informed him that she would be taking the boys to Manhattan. They planned to see an off-Broadway matinee, some farce about the French Revolution. He had lodged a tepid protest, "Are you sure decapitation is appropriate for third and fifth graders?"

"Kids see worse stuff on American TV," his wife assured him. "Besides, thousands of French children have seen it with no trauma reported." Already late for work that day, Will conceded. He trusted her judgment and left it at that.

Will walked into the kitchen, opened the refrigerator and pulled out a cold Rolling Rock. He then walked to the mailbox. In addition to the usual junk mail and bills, he found a post card with a beautiful image of

Lake Louise. It was from his mother who was on a two week Trailways Bus excursion with her friend, Betty.

But two additional pieces of correspondence demanded immediate attention: one from the office of the Superintendent of Schools where he taught, and the other from the Garden City law office of Heist, Lynch and Robb. Apprehensively, he walked back into the kitchen, sat down and opened the envelopes.

Getting fired from one's job and being served with divorce papers don't normally happen on the same day. Hence the scream.

On previous occasions, when confronted with possible problems regarding his teaching performance or in his marital relationship, Will had been loath to deal with the issues. Ofttimes he would point out the absurdity of any incriminations, then enter a state of denial. He reasoned that a shot across the bow isn't always followed by a broadside. When accused of being in denial, he would deny being in denial! What some saw as denial was simply his incurable optimism, he rationalized, his "glass is always half-full" outlook: a positive attribute. But could he really deny seeing these debacles coming? Not if he was honest.

Consider his marriage for example. Will should have been more mindful of the growing friction between him and his wife. He had been sensing it for some time, after all. There was that instance a while back when he had presented her with an exquisite wooden carving on the occasion of their tenth anniversary. Upon unwrapping the gift, she had seemed less than enthralled. A few weeks later he overheard Katie on the phone with her mother, "How can he not know that wood is for the fifth anniversary? It's diamonds for the tenth!"

He kept it to himself a few days before confronting her. "Diamonds? You were upset because you didn't get diamonds?"

"Well," Katie responded, "it's just that when you look these things up, they say diamonds...that or aluminum or tin...depending upon who's telling you."

"Exactly my point," Will replied. "Are you listening to yourself? Did it ever occur to you that these so-called 'traditional' gifts are actually not-so- cleverly disguised marketing ploys? Like the 'A Diamond is Forever' campaign years back that made them almost a necessity. Of course, inconvenient truths about violence, exploitation and human rights abuses in diamond mining operations are conveniently overlooked."

In reply, Katie shouted, "You are such a downer! More than that actually! You're a cynical, self-righteous bastard!"

An icy weekend had followed.

A similar episode had occurred just a month ago when Will and Katie were invited to a Cinco de Mayo party.

"Are they Mexican?", Will asked.

"The Collins'? I somehow doubt it. Why? Do you have to be Mexican? It's just a party," Katie argued.

"What's with this Cinco de Mayo stuff all of a sudden?" Will protested. "I don't get it! Neither do Mexicans, by the way—real ones—the ones that live in Mexico. It's supposed to celebrate a Mexican victory over the French. Big deal…everyone beats the French! And who really created the holiday? I'll tell you who. American beer companies, that's who!"

"There you go again with your self-righteous rant…"

"Self-righteous? Will interrupted. "You call me self-righteous? OK, guilty as charged if it means thinking celebrations should have some family or cultural significance! Maybe I just think Americans have a responsibility to know the truth behind some of our so-called traditions and the holidays we celebrate!"

"Don't lecture me…I'm not a sixteen-year old in your classroom!" Katie stormed out of the room.

Petty squabbles like this had been erupting with growing frequency, leaving Will with a disturbing sense of being out-of-sync. Little things were becoming big things, even the fact that Will squeezed toothpaste from the bottom and Katie from the middle. It didn't take a psychologist to figure out that the increasing triviality of their squabbles was not a good sign.

Getting sacked from his job came as less of a surprise. Unfortunately, Will cherished liberal political ideas, but taught in a conservative community. One incident in particular raised a shit storm.

During a recent homeroom, a student had remained seated while the class stood for The Pledge. Will decided to ignore the gesture, thinking it would be short-lived. When the student sat for the entire week, he recognized that the protest was for real. Wishing to avoid an unpleasant scene, he chose not to say anything in front of the class. But the following week the student continued to remain seated. After class one day, Will gave him an opportunity to explain his actions, in private.

The young man, Josh Radke, was an exemplary student. He consistently made honor roll, was active in extra curriculars, and in his senior year was an all-county wrestler. He had no recorded incidents of prior misbehavior. He had always been the perfect kid. Hanging over his head was that a "goody two shoes" reputation would be part of his legacy, though no one dared say that to his face. He felt a growing need to round out his high school career with an act of rebellion. Maybe cut a class just so he could say he once cut class. Or talk back to a teacher. Instead he chose to ignore the Pledge, an act of disobedience based on principle. His anti-authority stance would have integrity. That's how good a kid he was.

Will had known Josh from the day he entered high school and in many ways the young man reminded him of himself when he was a student.

After school, with just the two of them in the classroom, Josh explained that his refusal to stand was based upon his interpretation of the first amendment. He objected to the "under God" clause. It was obvious that he had done his homework.

"The original pledge didn't have those words", Josh said. Of course, Will already knew that.

He asked, "Josh, when exactly was that line inserted?"

"That's a trap, Mr. Kraft! If I don't get it right, you'll accuse me of sleeping during class." They both laughed.

"Did I actually give the date in class?"

"C'mon, Mr.K, you know you did: the year at least! It was in 1954 during the Cold War in response to the threat of godless communism. But here's something I'll bet you didn't know. Did you know that Francis Bellamy, the author of the original pledge, the one without the 'under God' line, was a Baptist minister? Despite that, he was a strong proponent of separation of church and state. Many historians think he probably would have disapproved of that clause. Kind of ironic, don't you think?"

"I confess...I did not know that!" Will admitted. "Listen Josh, there's something else you should know. The word has gotten out about you sitting during the pledge. A certain group of parents in the community have voiced their displeasure. Outrage, actually. They've spoken to the principal and to the superintendent of schools, and are asking why you're being allowed to get away with it. The superintendent is siding with the parents, and is already on the principal's case. I was called into the office yesterday. I faced a barrage of questions about why I'm not insisting that you stand. Furthermore, they want to know why I'm not disciplining you."

"Disciplining me— For what? Is there something in the school's Code of Conduct that I'm violating? Mr. K, the courts have already ruled that there is no constitutional requirement for students to recite the pledge. Heck, look at Jehovah's Witnesses!"

Josh thought for a moment. "Look Mr.K, I can request a switch into another homeroom if you want. I don't want you getting into trouble."

"And let some other teacher get into trouble?" Will responded. "Or worse, you land in a homeroom with a hard ass who will try to force you to stand? And when you don't, he charges you with insubordination? Let's just see what happens. Stay in my homeroom. These things have a way of blowing over. There's only six weeks of school left."

As an afterthought, Will asked, "By the way, where're you going to College?"

"University of Richmond," Josh said proudly. "Just found out over the weekend."

"Good choice!" Will concurred

Unfortunately, things did not blow over. Almost immediately after reporting back to his principal and superintendent about the meeting with Josh, curious things began to happen. Administrators started showing up in Will's classroom more often, usually unannounced. Observations, both planned and unplanned (what they called "pop-ins") became more frequent. Clearly, the last few violated the teacher's contract. From a consistent history of "exemplary", Will's evaluations declined to "unsatisfactory", and finally down to the dreaded "**fails to meet district expectations.**"

Will had reason to believe that they were out to get him. For good reason.

So the bad news didn't just come from out of the blue. The handwriting had been on the wall (and the chalkboard of the classroom...) for some time. Why the scream? Maybe it was simply the finality of seeing it all spelled out on embossed stationery.

Will walked into the dining area and slowly approached the three-tiered antique ice chest that had been repurposed into a liquor cabinet. He paused to look at it. In the early years of their marriage, he and Katie had lovingly restored the piece. That was back in that time when their love for one another made life's possibilities limitless. Who would end up with that treasure? So few of their belongings fit into a neat category, his or hers, mine or yours. It wasn't just the objects themselves, but the stories that went with them, stories of lives shared.

He opened the cabinet and reached for a bottle of bourbon, Blanton's Single Barrel, a gift received on his recent fortieth birthday. Then holding it in his hand, Will thought better of it. To drink when despondent was never a great idea. To choose an outrageously expensive bottle in which to drown one's sorrows would be plain foolish. He put it back and retrieved the Jack Daniels instead.

CHAPTER 2

A PLAN OF INACTION!

Will awakened at 5AM in the throes of a savage hangover. In German it's called *Katzenjammer (KOT-sen-yammer),* literally "cats wail or caterwaul", giving it an air of slapstick or farce. But this was no laughing matter! He forced down a bowl of oatmeal to buffer the four aspirin he had swallowed, followed by a quart of water. Then he made a silent vow to never touch demon alcohol again, even though he had been told that such vows were a warning sign that you were indeed an alcoholic.

Still lying on the couch, he glanced at the remaining few ounces of lovely amber liquid in the bottle of Jack. It had been sealed when he removed it from the liquor cabinet the night before. A few days later, Will would calculate what his blood alcohol level had been. Only then would it occur to him that the white light he saw in his "dream" that night had probably been a near- death experience.

After finishing his oatmeal, he disconnected the telephone, crawled into his bed and didn't wake up until four in the afternoon. Still groggy but at least somewhat functional, he made a pot of coffee and began to re-examine his future. He would try to speak with his wife. *Are you sure you want to go through with this…look at some of the married couples we know…they have truly dysfunctional relationships but are still together.* He already knew that Katie would turn that argument on its head, *yes…and look at them!*

Perhaps it was time for him to face the reality that the marriage had been moribund for some time. Still, the feeling of finality that the lawyer's letter delivered had so devastated him yesterday.

Will formulated a plan of action —some might say more a plan of "inaction"— but a vast improvement over the Jack Daniels strategy. He would drive down to Ponce de Leon Estates, Florida, where his parents Ernie and Lois had been living in retirement for the last five years. There he would break the news about his impending divorce and loss of job. He wanted to tell them in person. They were his parents after all, he owed them that much. After a day or so with his parents, he would light out for the territories: go off to Montana to seek solace in the wilderness and map out a real plan for the rest of his life.

But first he had something to take care of. The injustice of the dismissal from his teaching position had strengthened his resolve. He would fight this! He called the president of his teacher's union who gave him the name of the law firm that would assist him in the matter.

The next day Will sat in the lawyer's office with a dossier of documents. It included copies of the memoranda that had been exchanged between him and his principal and superintendent. Will had written evidence of everything: a paper trail. He had tape-recorded the conversations between him and the school administration. In addition, he also had recordings of discussions between himself and Josh Radke…with the permission of the student's parents, of course. He came with copies of all his lesson observations and performance reviews. The evidence pointed to a precipitous decline in his evaluations that suspiciously began at same time the fecal matter pertaining to the Pledge of Allegiance hit the fan.

Essentially, Will had already done the legal research into the matter for his attorney, but lawyers being lawyers, he knew they would never admit this. During the cursory examination of the documents in front of her, a smile crept across the lawyer's face. Noticing, Will thought to himself *I just hope this woman knows what she's doing!*

Following the visit with his attorney, Will returned home and prepared for the road trip. He packed a small suitcase, then organized his backpack with enough supplies for a seven day jaunt through the mountains. He filled his cooler with snacks and beverages and took a few minutes to replenish his CD case with new tunes and audio books. Everything went into the back of his twenty year old Astro Van. A week ago he had changed the oil and the engine's moving parts were now bathing happily in fresh Castrol full synthetic 10-30.

Will was fussy with the Astro. The reliable conveyance had chauffeured his boys' little league teams all over Long Island. It had been his daily commuter and had transported the family all over the country for vacations. The odometer was now approaching three hundred thousand, but it still ran perfectly.

In the faculty room Will once boasted that he planned to keep the car until it died a natural death. Then he would take all the money he saved and pay for his boys' college tuition. At that time, a local Long Island guy named Irv Gordon was gaining notoriety by logging over a million miles on his 1967 Volvo P-1800. Will had announced, "Hell, I could do that with the Astro...if I wanted!"

A contest began. Teachers being teachers, they started a pool. The art teacher rendered a line graph with help from a math teacher and hung it in the faculty room. Colleagues submitted twenty-dollar bills with their names and mileage predictions. Rules were drawn up. They allowed for one transmission repair or replacement, but no major engine overhaul. Will himself threw in twenty dollars with 500,000 K handwritten on the bill. The one who came closest to guessing the vehicle's mileage when it met its demise would take home $820.

He had taken the Florida trip so often...sometimes by himself, other times with friends, and most recently, with his wife and children... that he had become somewhat of an authority on driving to the Sunshine State. A "Roads Scholar" his colleagues dubbed him.

When friends and co-workers asked him for travel advice, Will was generous with his counsel. "Let me first tell you what NOT to do: Do not, under any circumstances...even if your kids plead with you... stop at "South of the Border" in South Carolina! Also, do not stop in chain pizza establishments! (but if in a moment of desperation, you should, and folks ask where're you're from, do not tell them you're from New York!) Finally, do not speed in the state of Georgia. Cops down there pull over cars with New York plates faster than you can say 'William Tecumseh Sherman!'"

The following morning at 2AM, Will cranked up the Astro and was on his way. He turned on the radio to his favorite station and on came Neil Young's "Long May You Run." Funny thing how omens always come when you least expect them and also when you need them most.

CHAPTER 3

I FELL IN LOVE WITH A LESBIAN GIRL

---∿---

Back in the Sixties (why do we love every story that begins with those words?), Scottish folk rocker "Donovan" (Donovan Philips Lietch) wrote a song "I Love My Shirt" in which appears the refrain:

> "I love my shirt, I love my shirt,
> My shirt is so com-fort-ab-ly-love-ly"

It's a fascinating thing, the alchemy of songwriting. Many fell in love with that quirky song. The lyrics are so relatable. Didn't we all own a shirt like that? The kind of shirt that elicits compliments: "Hey man, nice shirt!" But is such affirmation necessary? Isn't it really more of a personal thing between you and the shirt?

Will threw one of those shirts into his luggage. He had actually began rationing the times he wore it, not wishing to hasten its demise, and let's face it, nobody wants friends whispering behind their back, "He's not wearing that shirt…again?"

On the second night of his journey, Will did take that shirt out of his suitcase. He was planning to listen to some live music and not planning to dine on saucy cuisine that might forever compromise his shirt. It all came about when he was driving through Georgia and began to experience a serious case of Interstate numbness. The remedy? Exit on to some blue highways, America's back roads. Was it Ralph Waldo Emerson who first said, "It's not the destination, it's the journey"?

Shortly thereafter, he came upon a somewhat forlorn motel. Judging by the flickering neon "V CA CY" sign, it seemed to suit his budget. Being a Friday night, he asked the innkeeper if there was any live music nearby.

An hour later, Will was standing at a local roadhouse sipping his third glass of wine, a Willamette Valley Pinot Gris (no reds tonight!), when a perfect female stranger approached, "Hey, my friend and I were just admiring your shirt… it's so cool!"

"????!!!…Oh, this shirt? I like it because it's comfy", and almost immediately felt less than satisfied with that lame response. *How suave I would have seemed if I had had the presence of mind to respond with the refrain from the Donovan song… but that stuff only happens in the movies.* But after all, he was caught by surprise. To his credit, he did recover quickly enough to riposte, "Who's your friend? I'd like to buy you both a drink in recognition of your good taste!" She turned and pointed out a cute young lady who gave him a smile and one of those shy little waves that some women do so well.

A second look at his new friends quickly dispelled any misgivings he may have had about lesbian sartorial tastes. When he finally took the time to look closely at his surroundings, he had a startling realization. A eureka moment. He was in a lesbian bar!

Why he wasn't aware of this sooner is hard to say. Maybe the robust cannabis he had indulged in had clouded his perception, causing him to miss the subtle ten foot high neon sign announcing the name of the establishment: "Mons Venus". As for the bouncer at the entrance with the crew cut and tank top and muscular tattooed arms who proofed him before taking the ten dollar cover, she did sport impressive biceps… but Will simply thought to himself, "Wow, you've come a long way, baby!" He hadn't even picked up on the most obvious clue: his was the only car in the parking lot NOT a Subaru Forester! He was a Chevy in a Subaru bar! How did he not notice that? Maybe it was the distraction of the parking lot itself, a grove of massive live oaks draped in Spanish moss, so Southern Gothic and beguiling.

Too late now. To walk out over a feeling of slight discomfort would have sent the wrong message. And after all, he had promised the ladies a drink. And besides, and the most important reason of all, he found himself curiously attracted to the girl with the shy little wave...the one who liked his shirt. He always had this thing about lesbian girls, did Will. There was that infatuation with k.d. lang a while back...

So the girls got their drinks and promptly returned the favor and so did he, and so on and on throughout the evening. Will and his new friends properly monopolized the dance floor, especially when the band covered CCR's *Proud MARY*. And throughout the evening, Will searched the eyes of the young lady with the shy little wave, looking for a sign that she'd been miscast in her life role. That sign never came. As for his own role that night, he was content to play court jester in his cool shirt, so com-fort-ab-ly-love-ly.

At closing time, Will staggered into his Astro and wisely waited for the Subaru to parade out of the parking lot. He had time to kill and while sitting in the heat of that steamy Georgia night, the muses paid a visit. Had they been hiding all along in the Spanish moss and now sensed a troubled soul? Muses *are* attracted to broken hearts, that's a known fact. We'll never know for certain how it came to be, but before long there was a pen in his hand and some bar napkins came out of his pockets...it would have to do. *And muses were known to be somewhat capricious*, Will thought to himself, and so began writing.

Twenty minutes later he had something of which he was...well... quite proud. And not for the first time, he was astounded at the brilliant insights discovered under the influence of cannabis. His inner genius had been liberated! On those previous occasions, his delusions of adequacy were shattered upon the sober reflection of the following day. This time, he thought to himself...*it would be different*!

The band, which it should be mentioned, went by the name of *The Mysterious Mudpuppies*, had broken down their equipment. The musicians were enjoying a well-earned drink at the bar with the proprietress of "Mons Venus". As Will re-entered, the lead vocalist and head mudpuppy, Tommy

13

Lee Clarke, recognized him: "Well looky, looky...if it ain't the dancin' fool!"

"Never mind...'dancin' fool! I'm here on business!" Will held up the crumbled wet napkin. But I'm not adverse to mixing business with pleasure as long as I'm not asked to pay for my beverage because I believe that might be a violation of the ABC board. While I'm enjoying a glass of your finest Pinot Gris, take a look at this and tell me what you think." He handed the napkin to Tommy Lee.

"Whatchugotthere?" holding the wet napkin at a distance, squinting.

"A little something I wrote in the parking lot ...apologies for the stationery. Since you guys are part of the inspiration behind it, I thought I'd give you first dibs before it gets picked up by *Alabama* or *The Oak Ridge Boys* or some other band with fame and fortune that doesn't need the money."

And so they all huddled around and managed to decipher the following:

> *Lesbian Girl Blues*
> *I know you think you're a lesbian girl*
> *But would you consider giving me a whirl?*
> *Whatever may be your persuasion,*
> *Maybe on this one occasion?*
> *Not looking to make a conversion,*
> *Thought maybe just a diversion?*
> *I can take no for an answer,*
> *But I bet you're a real good dancer*
> *And I'd like to do it...real slow*
> *No matter what happens tonight...*
> *Lord I know this is not right...*
> *I'm not sure what the point is I'm makin'*
> *But will you leave me with my heart breakin'?*

Will then finished his final glass of wine, and handed the boys his business card. He slowly turned, wobbled back to his car and drove back to the motel. A self-satisfied grin crept across his face. After all, had he not just made a lasting contribution to the Great American Song Book?

CHAPTER 4

PONCE DE LEON ESTATES, FLORIDA.

---◇---

On his sagging mattress, Will rolled over to check the alarm clock. It confirmed what he already knew. He would not be getting an early start today.

The shower provided balm for the second worst hangover in less than a week. No "hair-of-the-dog" this morning. His first stop would be the Waffle House and its endless cups of coffee. After his fifth cup, the waitress quipped, "Hon, I think we're losin' money on you," but it was said ever so kindly. *Ah, the South, where the waitresses call you 'Hon' and young men address you as 'Sir'*

"Don't you worry, sweetie," replied Will sheepishly, "I'll be sure to show my appreciation when we reckon the bill. By the way, could you fill the thermos please?" he asked, definitely pushing his luck.

He made his way back to the parking lot, climbed into the Astro and popped in a Ray Charles CD, the one with "Georgia on My Mind"(*When in Rome…)* and was on his way.

It's been said bad things happen in threes. Sure enough, somewhere south of Sarasota, so tantalizingly close to his destination, the transmission began to slip. Then the faithful 4.3 liter V-6 started to sound like a diesel…

which it wasn't. In addition to getting divorced and fired, Will could now add mechanical problems to his woes.

His friends had warned him about the lack of judgement in setting off on a ten thousand mile road trip from New York to Florida to Montana and back in a vehicle with 300,000 ticks on the odometer. But he would prove them wrong. Now this!

Will pulled off the highway to check lubricant levels. Tranny and engine were both full. Bad news! It meant a more sinister explanation lay behind the slippage and under- hood rattling. Knowing that his parents lived only twenty miles away, he decided to chance it. So he put the flashers on and drove real slow, when necessary waving other drivers on or using the shoulder of the road.

An hour later he arrived at Ponce deLeon Estates. At the entrance, he provided ID to the uniformed guard, who remarked contemptuously, "She's making quite a racket...engine problems?" Will ignored the comment and headed off to his parents.

Ponce de Leon's search for the so-called "Fountain of Youth" was most certainly apocryphal. This fact did nothing to deter the diaspora of folks fleeing the cold winters of the upper Midwest and high taxes of the Northeast to stake out their little piece of paradise in the Sunshine State. In fact, many of them were now peeking out their doors wondering where the racket was coming from.

Will finally limped into his parents' driveway. His dad, Ernie, was already out the door, alarmed at what he thought was a cement-mixer on the premises. Will quickly shut off the engine and jumped out with a celebratory, "I made it!" Then he propped up the hood.

"So she finally quit on you!" said Ernie, stating the obvious.

"Doesn't sound good, does it? Maybe we can get a tow truck to come to the trailer park."

His father was always quick to remind anyone (including his son) who dared refer to Ponce deLeon Estates as a "trailer park" that they were in error. "It's a 'luxury manufactured home community'!"

"What's the difference again, Dad...I forgot."

Each time his dad would explain the subtle distinctions, and each time it was something different. This time he said, "I'll take you to a 'trailer park' and then you tell me the difference! First of all, people in trailer parks smoke cigarettes and listen to Hillbilly music! Secondly, they don't go on the courts and whup their disrespectful sons in tennis!"

"That hurt, Dad!"

"And another thing, trailer-park-folks drive twenty year old Chevies that are constantly breaking down!"

"...and that hurt even more!"

Then they promptly laughed and gave each other a big hug, and in no time at all, Will's mom, Lois, joined in the love fest.

Ernie assured his son that "good, honest mechanic" was not an oxymoron. In fact, his name was Bruno and his shop was nearby.

A half hour later, Bruno's son, Vincent, showed up in a tow truck, all chrome and bright cherry red. The Astro was towed away for a diagnosis, and hopefully not a post-mortem. Not wishing to incur the wrath of silver-haired vigilantes, Vincent was careful to keep his truck at a speed well below the posted **"Slow: 14 miles per hour!"**

Nonetheless, the excitement was enough to get some of the residents to step out of their luxury manufactured homes to gawk and then talk.

Lars Johansson from Minnesota, Fritzie Emmerich from Milwaukee and Paddy McCann recently out of Elizabeth, New Jersey quickly formed a trio.

"That's why I don't buy a General Motors product" volunteered Lars.

"My fifteen year old Mercury Marquis has thirty thousand miles on it and still runs like a charm!", boasted Fritz.

"Hold on," protested Paddy. "My Pontiac Aztec is a terrific car!"

"Yah," quipped Lars. "But it's so ugly, that it has to sneak up to a gas pump!" The teasing went on for a while until air-conditioning once again beckoned.

And so it goes. Legions of refugees from the North hunkering behind the defensive perimeters of gated Floridian communities designed to ward off the menace of an increasingly hostile outside world, and each day another day in paradise!

Then Will remembered that he had driven to Florida to share his misfortunes. The longer he waited, the more difficult it would be. What

Will did not know is that his parents, especially Mom, had been sensing problems with the marriage for the past several years. The discussion took place over a fresh pot of coffee and an Entenmann's Walnut Danish Ring. It lasted well over an hour and a few tears were shed, first by Lois, then by Will. Ernie took a brief walk outside to "get some fresh air". When Will looked out the window, he saw his father leaning against the storage shed, wiping his eyes. *At least he can still say he never cried in front of his son.*

Over the past five years, Will had visited his folks on several occasions, always with Katie and the boys. Those were fun times, and of course, Eric and Paul always returned home properly spoiled. Lois was a great cook and would truly rise to the occasion for her grandchildren. These visits included the typical Florida pastimes of swimming in the community pool and playing shuffleboard. They would also go fishing, explore the local beaches and of course, take the obligatory trip to Disney World. A confirmed iconoclast, Will was a member of that small minority of Americans that snubbed Mickey and his loony cohorts. Oh, he would visit the theme park with the family, and he would even get some pleasure out of it (something he never admitted…) but it was mainly pleasure of a vicarious sort through his children.

More often he would express bemusement at the fact that full-grown adults would visit Disney…without children! That folks actually made arrangements to have weddings here was beyond his comprehension. His most scathing derision, however, was reserved for Americans who would travel all the way to Europe to visit…*Disneyland Paris!*

Mostly Will enjoyed seeing his parents. He also loved Florida for its natural beauty, but lamented how pristine areas were being swallowed up by developers and replaced with gated communities ironically named after what had been bulldozed: places like "Quail Ridge", "Panther Key" and "Fox Hunt Pines." They surely had a knack for paving paradise and putting up a parking lot!

Whenever Mom had Will alone for a minute, she would provide him with the latest health updates. "I think your dad is getting hard of hearing."

"What makes you say that, Mom?"

"Well, the other day we were returning home from a little gathering at the neighbor's. He turns to me and asks, "What did you mean when you asked me, 'Did you join the Y'? Why would I join the Y? I get enough exercise with my tennis and bike riding!' I looked at him and said 'Hon, I asked, Did you *enjoy the wine*?' That sort of thing is happening more and more..."

"Write them all down, mom! I see a funny book coming out of this!"

The day after Will arrived, the strangest thing happened. He had gone into the tool shed to locate a pair of needle-nose pliers for a quick repair on his backpack. Behind the tool box, he uncovered a cache of photos: 8 x 10 glossies featuring well-turned ladies legs and feet adorned in very attractive footwear, mostly of the high heeled stiletto type.

As Will was going through the photos, he heard his dad's voice, "Find the pliers?" and in another second he's in the shed. Of course, realizing that Will had already made the discovery, there was little he could do? "Jeez... don't tell your mother about those pictures! I hid them behind the tools because she never comes in here."

Will had no choice but to confront his father. "So tell me what's going on here, Dad...I won't judge."

His dad first stammered a bit before coming out with something about how when a man reaches a certain age he might need a little help in the libido department, and after an awkward minute or so, somewhat desperately exclaimed, "I can't believe I'm discussing these things with my grown ..."

Will cut him off. "I said I won't judge!

"So I guess what I'm saying is that ladies' shoes for whatever reason do a little something for me and your mom in the bedroom department...if you know what I mean."

"Mom knows nothing about this?"

"Not about the pictures, she doesn't! You think they would be hidden in the tool shed if she did?"

"Don't worry, Dad! I can keep a secret. But aren't you a little old to suddenly develop a... foot fetish?"

"Jeez, don't use that word!"

"What, 'old'?" replied Will.

"No, not 'old'! Hell, I know I'm old. It's that 'fetish'word! Makes me sound like a pervert or sex fiend! But I will admit, these things probably don't happen to most men in their seventies."

"Dad, anyone else know about this shoe thing?"

"Only Pete (Pete Magee was dad's regular tennis doubles partner). But he's got some funny things going on himself!" He then continued his explanation to his son. "This shoe thing spices up my sex life more than any Viagra…"

But Will had no desire to hear anything further on the icky subject of his parents' sex life. He was losing his patience. "OK dad, that's great, but do I really have to hear about this part of your life? Do you really need to be sharing this with me?"

At that moment, Will was overcome by a terrifying thought, the kind that could possibly lead to nightmares. For the past few months, his father had been talking about getting a part-time job nearby. What if he got a sales job in a women's' shoe boutique over in Sarasota and wound up getting led away in handcuffs by some mall cop for inappropriate behavior? And it wound up on the local new channel. On the other hand, thought Will, maybe that's what he needed. Not a sex offender arrest, of course, but a job that would immerse him into the world of bunions, hammertoes, malodorous feet and varicose veins. Maybe that would rid him of his affliction.

The following day, a call came from dad's mechanic, Bruno. Ernie put his son on the phone. "I've got some good news, and I've got some bad news." *Why do repairmen and mechanics always start out with that… is that something they're taught in trade school?*

"Let's hear it, Bruno."

"Well, you're definitely in need of a new transmission. I can get you a rebuilt one. It'll run about three thousand dollars with labor. The engine noise turned out to be a minor issue and should come in under a hundred dollars."

"Bruno, was that the good news or the bad?"

"Hah! I see you got your dad's sense of humor. That was the good news!"

"I was afraid of that. What's the bad?"

"Well, if you want to go ahead with the transmission…I'm only asking because I see that bad boy's got three hundred and one thousand on the odometer…we can do it, but the car won't be ready for three weeks…"

"Three weeks?"

"Three weeks. I tried all over to get a tranny sooner, …but…"

Will thought about it. Then he thought about the faculty room pool (if he would ever step foot in that room again was entirely another matter…) and how he boasted to his co-workers that he would get 500K on the Astro, and how the money saved would go towards his kids' college tuition… "OK, Bruno, go ahead with it!"

Of course, now there remained another issue: how to get to Montana? He had promised his family that he would be back in New York in less than a month. That he was going to "See the U-S-A in his Chev-Ro-Lay".

It was at that moment that he came up with a brilliant idea. A "Plan B". He would **hitchhike** to Montana!

Scratching his head, Will thought, *Maybe that's what life is after all. One big 'Plan B'!*

CHAPTER 5

A WORD OR TWO ABOUT HITCHHIKING

Hitchhiking, was it legal or illegal? Most say illegal. Even many police officers. Let's set the record straight. It is **legal** in most places, provided it's done correctly. More on the legality later...

Will had considerable experience with hitchhiking. Since the age of twelve, he had many occasions to thumb a ride, and since he began driving legally, he himself had himself picked up many a soliciter (*soliciting a ride* is how most vehicle codes refer to hitchhiking). It's safe to say that anyone who has ever stood along side the highway, pollex extended, was himself more likely to pick up hitchhikers. Empathy comes from life experiences.

Over the years, Will had picked up college students and high school drop-outs, soldiers and peaceniks, an Irish waitress and a German exchange student, a Mormon and a Hasidic Jew. He had given lifts to those with broken down cars and to others with broken down lives. There were drunks who couldn't afford another DWI.

As a hitchhiker, he had gotten lifts from men and women (in retrospect, far too few women), African- Americans and full blood Indians. Traveling salesmen seemed to pick up hitchhikers quite often: one sold vacuum cleaners and another specialized in large agricultural metal barns. There was even a guy who sold bibles. He claimed to have five hundred of The Good Books in the trunk of his car. There was the overly amorous gay guy who kept commenting on the size of Will's hands...Will bailed out of that car at the first opportunity!

In Montana one time, he had been given a ride by a preacher who had a taxidermy business on the side (or was the side business his ministry?). He was driving a '55 Studebaker, one of six that he owned. Shit-kickers had given him rides as well as urban sophisticates.

Maybe it wasn't Emerson who first said, "It's not the Destination, it's the journey". Maybe those were the words of a hitchhiker. Maybe the great American philosopher was himself a hitchhiker.

Will had many hitchhiking stories. He was once given a ride by a fellow whose claim to fame was being a "milk-carton kid" back in the 80s. That was the era when all over the country, faces of adorable "missing" children were plastered on milk containers. Americans learned that they were in the midst of a kidnapping epidemic.

"'I was five years old,' explained the fellow, 'sitting at the kitchen table enjoying a bowl of Cocoa Puffs. My mother was reading the paper while nibbling on an English muffin and smoking her first Virginia Slim of the day. I was staring at the milk carton when it dawned on me that the kid on the carton was ME! With a different last name, but most definitely me.'"

"'Mom,' I said, 'that kid on the container looks like me! He even has the same birthday!' I pushed the milk carton toward my mom and urged her to take a look.

"'My mother scrutinized the picture, read the information, then looked at me and asked, 'Billy, do you know where you are?'"

"'Of course I do,' I replied."

"'Well so do I. So you are definitely not missing. It should be your father's picture on there. He's been missing in action for most of your life! Now go ahead and finish your Cocoa Puffs!'"

There's the widely held belief that hitchhiking is dangerous, that there are weirdos and homicidal maniacs out there. Of course, Will didn't want to die at the hands of a homicidal maniac. His preference was at the age of a hundred, in his sleep, maybe in a nursing home spooning his twenty year old nurse.

Will had studied statistics in college. He understood probability. That's why he avoided those robbers of youth, cigarettes and overeating and tried his best to stay in shape. That's why he was willing to board an airplane and willing to swim in oceans filled with sharks. It was why he was willing to step out of his house each day and cross the street. It was also why he was willing to occasionally hitchhike.

Hitchhikers are a tribe of optimists.

Indeed, it could even be said that hitchhiking has enriched our lives. Consider music, cinema and literature. We wouldn't have Kris Kristofferson's gem, "Me and Bobby McGee", where "Bobby thumbed a diesel down, just before it rained..." We also wouldn't have that hilarious scene in the movie, "Five Easy Pieces", where Jack Nicholson picked up two hitchhiking girls, and one of them went on a hilarious rant about all the crap and filth in the world. Of course, let's not forget one of America's literary greats, Jack Kerouac. He and hitchhiking are practically synonymous.

Back in his younger days when he was hitching more often, Will had photocopied and laminated that portion of the NYS Vehicle Code that addressed the subject: **Title 7 Rules of the Road, Article 27, #1157. Pedestrians soliciting rides...(a) No person shall stand in a roadway for the purposes of soliciting a ride (hitchhiking)**

The key words are "...stand in the roadway...". The fact is that just about everywhere, soliciting a ride (hitchhiking) is not illegal as long as the person is not standing on the roadbed. Not allowing the hitchhiker to *stand in the roadway* makes perfectly good sense. Standing on the shoulder or beyond leaves one perfectly within his rights.

Of course standing alongside any limited access highway like Interstates or toll roads, is just about always illegal. Here you stick your thumb out on entrance ramps or at rest stops.

On one or two occasions, Will actually did need to produce that laminated document (which he kept tucked away in his backpack). By doing so, he was able to remind overly zealous police officers that by standing on the shoulder, he was in compliance with the vehicle code. One young officer radioed his superior to confirm. Upon confirmation, he went on his way.

In South Dakota, on another occasion, the officer told him,"I don't care what the law says, I want you off the highway immediately!"

"You say 'I don't care what the law says' replied Will incredulously. A law enforcement agent who doesn't care what the law is!?" One look at the officer's scowl suggested that it was best not to take it any further. "OK then…I'll walk to Montana…"

Will had nine college psychology credits under his belt. But he intuitively knew that folks naturally gravitate toward someone with a sense of humor. So before embarking on any journey which might necessitate "soliciting a ride", he would sometimes take along a huge, bright yellow "thumbs up" hand (such gimmicks once served as soft-drink promotional material). The inspiration for that foam-rubber prosthesis came from Sissy Hankshaw, the inveterate hitchhiker with freakishly large thumbs in Tom Robbins' **Even Cowgirls Get the Blues.** Will could see the smiles on the face of motorists, even the many that sped right by.

As his hitchhiking experiences accumulated, Will learned to turn down rides for strategic purposes. For example, sometimes a driver would say that he'd give you a lift, but he was only going a few miles down the road, would that help? It might be best to decline that offer. Unless, of course, it took you to a major intersection that would increase the odds of getting a better lift. There's strategy involved. Which is why some call it "the art of hitchhiking".

Let's say you do get a ride, and it's going to be a long one. On such occasions, it would be a good idea to offer to pay part of the gas expenses or to buy lunch or dinner or even help with the driving. Little gestures pay big dividends! On one occasion, Will offered to share driving and gas with a traveling salesman. That one ride took him four hundred and eighty five miles, a distance greater than the width of North Dakota.

Will knew two more strategies. First, although it may be stating the obvious, one must "dress for success". Appearance counts! Secondly, and this strategy Will had personally field- tested: carry a sign! A sign informs folks that you, the hitchhiker, are goal-oriented and responsible. Will would always pack along a few blank pieces of 10" x 18" oak tag and a permanent magic marker on which to write his destinations.

On the morning he stood along the entrance ramp on I-75 in Florida, did he actually write **"MONTANA"** on his sign? Of course not. He chose a modest and attainable destination, **"ST PETE",** about thirty miles north. Once in St. Petersburg, he could always make another sign, perhaps **"OCALA"**. The object is to get someone to pull over, and to get into the car. The "foot-in-the-door" concept. You could always feel things out to see if the driver was receptive to taking you further.

The following morning, Will's strategies actually did pay off!

CHAPTER 6

CROSS THAT BRIDGE WHEN WE GET TO IT

———————cﬗɔ———————

"Throw your stuff in the back and hop in!" Will's "stuff" consisted of a backpack, a small suitcase and a tall wooden hiking stick that went with him on all his treks into the wild.

"Nice Buick" said Will as he slid into the passenger seat of an early 1980s Electra Estate Wagon. Though the vehicle was almost twenty years old, it was mint. When getting picked up, Will would always start with a compliment just to make sure things get off to a good start.

"People say it looks like that station wagon the Griswolds drove in that first vacation movie," said the driver. Will took a moment to look at her as she eased the station wagon onto the entrance ramp. She was attractive, obviously athletic. Probably in her mid-thirties. Her wavy brunette hair had a casual, no-frills look, and if she wore make-up at all, it wasn't obvious.

"You must mean the 'Wagon Queen Family Truckster Station Wagon'!" asserted Will.

"Oh my god! You know that? I can't believe you actually know that!"

"What was the name of the dog... the one tied to the car by its leash that they dragged?" As soon as she asked, she turned around and addressed the dog in the back seat. "Walter, close your ears...don't listen to this!"

Up until then, Will hadn't noticed the tan, medium-sized, mixed breed pooch curled up in the back seat. But he continued, "I remember what the cop said: 'Poor little guy…probably kept up with you for a mile or so… tough little mutt!'"

"Stop it! I get so angry with myself whenever I laugh at that scene!"

Will went on. "His name was Dinky, by the way."

When the laughter subsided, Annie introduced herself. "I'm Annie… Annie Arnold."

"And I'm Will Kraft."

"With a 'K' or a 'C'?"

"Kraft with a 'K'," replied Will, secretly appreciating the fact that she requested that detail.

"You really want to know about this Buick? I know it has that old people's car reputation. You probably think it's my dad's car, maybe my grandfather's."

"Since you brought it up, not too many people your age are driving Buicks… any model year. By the way, I'll bet you didn't know that more Buicks are sold in China than America."

"Of course I knew that," she insisted.

Will now realized there was nothing more he could contribute on the subject of Buicks, so he let his driver do most of the talking.

Which she was more than willing to do: "Why not a Buick…I was conceived in the backseat of a '56 Roadmaster, if family lore is reliable."

Not much he could say to that, so Will filled in the awkward pause by looking over his shoulder to check out her dog, definitely no AKC recognized breed, but a handsome fellow with a doleful countenance. "Nice pooch!"

"Where I go, he goes. You think I'd pick somebody up …no offense, you look like a nice enough guy…but do you think I would have picked you up if Walter…his name is Walter after my favorite uncle…if Walter was not with me? You're obviously not afraid of dogs…some people are I know, which I don't quite understand, but then again who am I to judge. I have this weird thing called gephyrophobia …don't ask me to spell it. It's a fear of driving over bridges. I should say, I *had* that phobia. Walter has been a big help in that department although he's not what you call a therapy dog …at least not officially registered as one."

"Walter cured you?"

"Let me tell you what happened." Annie spoke in that non-accent of the midwestern educated class. Will found her voice, with its contralto-like quality, rather soothing. "A few years ago, I was approaching that long bridge that takes you into St Pete, with Walter sitting right where you are. Based upon my personal history, I wasn't so sure I could make it. I decided on a pedal-to-the-metal strategy. By the way, I owned an old Volvo 240 at the time, so pedal-to-the-metal wasn't quite as risky as it sounds. I figured the quicker I crossed the bridge, the less time to panic and hyperventilate. So I glanced over at Walter and said, 'here goes!' In that very moment I beheld in that dog's face a look of pure joy … serenity actually… and an epiphany took place … in me… not Walter: if Walter had no problem with bridges, 'and no offense, honey (she was addressing her dog, apologetically), but I think I'm at least as smart as you are', then why on earth should I be having these stupid anxiety attacks? It was that simple!"

Annie continued. "So Walter is not only my quadruped friend and soul mate, but my therapist. Sometimes I think he might even be my spiritual advisor … and I mean that! You see at the time of this bridge epiphany, I had been seeing a shrink for over a year to help me deal with my divorce. The bridge thing happen to come up a few times. During one of our sessions, I also shared that piece of information about being conceived in the back of a Buick…don't ask me why that came up. My psychologist concluded that the event —the back seat event—was the source of my phobia and my feelings of self-loathing and worthlessness. He advised me to sell my Volvo. How he knew I had a Volvo, I have no idea. Maybe he saw me pull into the parking lot. Anyway, he instructed me to sell the Volvo and buy a Buick. It would be the first step toward confronting those issues caused by the circumstances of my conception.'"

"I told him that I had never thought of myself as insecure, or that I loathed myself. *Up until then, that is.* Of course not, he said. He then proceeded to explain the insidious nature of repression.

So I just bought this Buick even though I really loved my Volvo ... do you know how difficult it is to part with a car that you have given a name to...Vivian the Volvo? By the way, are you from New York? You sound like you're from New York. Do you know about that guy, Irv Gordon, who has over a million miles on his old Volvo...or is it three million? He does advertisements for Volvo? "He's from New York, too." She caught herself and apologized for digressing.

"Actually, I do know about Irv Gordon...but tell me more about the Buick."

"So anyway, I sold Vivian and bought this Buick from an older gentleman who lived in that big retirement community down near Fort Myers... Sunset Palms Vista something or other. It's an OK car...actually a real cream puff with only 43,000 miles, but I still haven't come up with a name for it...or is it a 'her'...why are cars always feminine...?"

"What about the bridge phobia and the therapy with your shrink? I don't think you really finished explaining that."

"You're right. Because I had already made a commitment of sorts, I decided to stick out the therapy and continued to spend many sessions exploring those feelings of self- loathing and worthlessness that I had no idea I had, resulting from my haphazard conception in the back of a Roadmaster. That was the model my parents owned. You could tell one Buick from another back then by the number of portholes. Do you know how many portholes a Roadmaster had back in 1956? Four. The Roadmaster had four and cheaper models like the Special only had three. I'm not digressing... you probably think I am. Believe it or not, as a part of my therapy, I was assigned by Murray...my therapist was Doctor Murray Freudenberg, but he said it was OK to just call him 'Murray'. ..I think he had been a hippie back in the sixties. Anyway, Murray gave me an assignment to do research on all things Buick. He said it was a way of 'confronting the underlying and repressed source' of my problem. 'Based on the trauma of your conception,' he told me, 'it would be remarkable if you were *NOT* bridge phobic!'"

"Of course, after Walter cured me of my phobia, I started to regret having sold the Volvo.

All along, I thought that Murray's theory about my bridge fears being caused by my conception in the back of a Buick was a bit of a stretch. After all, a lot of people are conceived in the back seats of cars. They don't all become bridge phobic, or phobic in any way. But a lot of the other stuff he was telling me actually did make sense. Unfortunately, none of the psychological mumbo-jumbo fixed the bridge thing. In the final analysis, that was Walter.

She turned her head once again, and asked her dog in that cutesy way people talk to their pets, "Wasn't it you who helped Momma?"

"Anyway," she continued, "after Walter cured me, I had to call up Dr. Freudenberg to tell him I no longer required his services, but thanks for everything. I also assured him that I didn't loathe myself as much any more. Of course, I didn't say anything about Walter. For a short while, Murray was quiet on the other end of the phone. He then asked me, 'Would you mind telling me something, and I promise I won't take offense. Are you seeing someone else?'"

"The way he asked made him sound more like a boyfriend who's being dumped rather than a shrink, or maybe that was just my take. But anyway, I decided to tell him....sort of that is."

I said, "Actually, there is. His name is Walter."

There was another pause before Murray pleaded, "Please tell me it's not Walter_____!"

"And here I forget the last name, but it was one of those names you see on shingles all over the place, something 'berg or stein' ... but he needed to know if it was Dr Walter Somethingberg, and the tone of his voice told me he would have been highly offended, professionally speaking I guess, if it had been. I actually heard an audible sigh of relief from him when I answered, 'No, just Doctor Walter. Someone you never heard of.'

"Can you imagine his reaction if I had told him the real truth about my dog curing me?"

There was a lengthy pause before Annie spoke again. "Your sign says 'St. Pete', Will. What are you doing there?"

"Actually, I'm on my way to Montana, but if I held up a sign saying 'Montana', people might get scared or think I'm crazy."

"You think they'd be afraid of you?"

"What, you don't think so? Who hitches all the way to Montana?" Will then went on to explain the present circumstances of his life: the divorce, getting sacked from his teaching position and the decision to light out for the territories and seek balm in the wilderness. It probably took a good half hour of explaining what with all her questions.

Just how Annie would process all this information was a big unknown for Will. The last thing he needed from her was pity. She had been rather forthcoming with him in the little time they had shared. She certainly didn't appear to be the judgmental type. On the contrary, she responded with unexpected empathy

"Actually," said Annie, "I'm on my way to Austin, Texas. I recently moved back there to live with my parents while I work out issues having to do with my own divorce. I work for an educational publishing company and just spent a few days at a conference in Tampa. I flew here from Austin, but now I'm driving this Buick back, which by the way has yet to be named, so if you have any ideas, I'm open for suggestions.

A short pause followed before Annie continued. "If you don't mind sharing the driving, I can take you to Texas. I was going to make it in three days, but if you're up for it, with the two of us doing the driving, we can get to Austin in much less time. We can take turns. You can sleep while I drive. I don't mind."

"Like the Melissa Etheridge song…"

"You know that song!?"

"Speaking of driving," Will added with some urgency, "you realize that you don't have a full tank of gas…in fact, it looks like it's on empty!"

"Oh my God…I hope we make it… I must not have been paying attention. This beast sure uses fuel…"

"Move over to the right lane, drop down to fifty five and get off at the next exit. I think I saw a sign for a gas station."

Annie coasted off the exit and barely made it to a gas station a half mile down the road. Will thought he heard the engine sputter as they pulled up to the pump.

"I got this one," offered Will, "That's the least I can do."

"Thanks," said Annie. "I've got to use the bathroom. You want a coffee or anything?"

"Small, dark, one sugar."

While in the convenience store gas station, Annie went looking through the vast array of snacks and candy bars without finding what she was looking for. So she asked the young man behind the cash register.

"You'll never find them," the young man replied. "Follow me…it's easier if I just take you to them. We had a young girl working for us who couldn't get the hang of the job… the artistic type with incredible tattoos, but a bit too creative when it came to stocking shelves. We had to let her go a few weeks back, but I'm still finding stuff in unlikely places. That candy bar you're looking for is mixed in with the fuel additives."

Despite his Shmoo-like physique, the young man was surprisingly light on his feet and whisked Annie off to the hidden stash in no time at all.

"Thanks, I never would have found them on my own."

A few minutes later, she came back out balancing a Skor Bar on top of two coffee cups. "Take either cup," she said, "I drink coffee the same as you do. You want half the Skors?"

"You're kidding, right?"

"Kidding? What do mean, kidding?"

"How'd you know Skors was my favorite…that or a Heath Bar?"

"You're just sayin' that, aren't you?" laughed Annie.

"Why would I make that up. I'm serious, Those two brands or a nice dark chocolate is all I ever buy, when I do buy candy."

"By the way, how much gas did she take?" wondered Annie.

"About twenty five gallons… I lost track."

"The tank's supposed to hold twenty four!"

"Close call," said Will, "we could have been alongside the highway for a while…"

"Maybe it's our lucky day." Replied Annie. Will thought he detected a coy smile.

"Another thing," added Will, "While filling the tank, I came up with a name for your car."

"Really? Let's hear it!"

"Beulah! Beulah, the Buick!"

"I love it."

35

CHAPTER 7

THE BIBLE SALESMAN
AND OTHER TALES
OF THE ROAD

The ride to Austin was going to be a blast. A decision was made to not rely on the interstate highways but enjoy some side excursions on blue highways. To travel like Walt Whitman and "hear America singing". The very first stop was St.Petersburg, Florida to have lunch out at the end of the long fishing pier jutting out into Tampa Bay. While walking on the pier they came upon the disturbing sight of a fisherman leaning over the rail with his butt crack in full glory.

"Did you ever wonder what plumbers do on their day off?" he asked Annie.

As she convulsed in laughter, folks on the pier began to stare. Will stepped away. *I have no idea who this person is* was the message, but secretly he was flattered by the notion of a woman appreciating his humor. His wife (ex-wife?) hadn't laughed at his jokes in years.

Soon they got back in the Buick continuing north on I-75. Every few hours, they took a pit stop and gave Walter some exercise. Conversation covered the gamut: family matters, friends, favorite foods, college experiences, politics and the old standbys of ethnic heritage and religion.

For whatever reason, they dwelled a long time on the topic of religion. Annie had a somewhat Roman Catholic upbringing, due largely to her mother's insistence, though Annie herself no longer subscribed. Will talked about his Lutheran upbringing, and how he had always felt an underlying tension between the teachings of Martin Luther and the streak of agnosticism and free-thinking on both sides of his lineage.

"These days I don't adhere to any organized religion," he admitted. "I'm more a fan of the dis-organized type. Think about it. Under the banner of god, people have justified slavery, disproportionately cruel punishments for minor offenses, not to mention persecution of those with non-conforming lifestyles."

"Do most folks really know what the Ten Commandments say? Will challenged. "Hell, Atheists and Agnostics never fought a Thirty Years War, never launched a crusade or jihad and never viewed themselves as a 'chosen people', because think about it... for agnostics, who would do the 'choosing'?"

The subject of divorce also came up. Annie's five- year marriage had ended almost a year ago. Will brought up his own marital situation. For him, at least up until recently, divorce was something that always happened to other people, like a terminal illness or fatal accident.

"Not so long ago," said Will, "I met an acquaintance I hadn't seen in a while, and he immediately shares with me that he and his wife are breaking up. Caught me by surprise. I mean, do I offer condolences or congratulations? So I asked him."

"What did he say?"

"It's cool," he said. "It's cool."

"What about you," said Annie. "Are you 'cool' with your own situation?"

The truth was that the thought of divorce from Katie weighed heavily upon him. "Quite frankly, I'm bummed out by the fact that my wife of fifteen years, the one that promised to love and cherish me till 'death do us part', is now determined to divorce me."

"Do you know the 'Serenity Prayer'?" Annie asked. "Oh, I forgot, Agnostics don't pray..."

"No… I know it. About being granted the serenity to accept the things you cannot change, the courage to change the things you can and the wisdom to know the difference…yeah, I know it. I'm still working on the 'wisdom' part."

An unwritten covenant was developing between Will and Annie. The abiding theme was safety. Safety in knowing that the sharing of their foibles and weaknesses would not end in exploitation. Will wondered where the boundary was, and how he would know when he reached it.

He continued to bare his soul. He heard himself using the term 'shameful" several times as he described his feelings about being involved in a divorce. He described not just a feeling of failure, but failure on a monumental scale. And not just failure in marriage, but failure as a person. He wondered if he would be able to pick up the pieces, and like a jigsaw puzzle, reassemble the pieces of himself into something coherent. But with a jigsaw, a picture of the final product is provided. How do you reassemble yourself as a person when you have no idea what you should look like? Do you just go back to being the same flawed human as you were before?

At some point during this conversation, his thoughts turned to Schopenhauer's "Hedgehog Dilemma", the metaphor about the difficulties of human intimacy: the closer a hedgehog gets to its partner in an effort to seek warmth, the greater the likelihood of harm. Will wondered if he was getting too close to Annie, too soon. Maybe it was time to change the subject.

Conveniently, a rest area came up. It was time for a break.

When the got back into the car, Annie started the conversation. She too had sensed that it was time to move on to a different topic. Something *lighter.* "So you must meet some interesting folks while hitchhiking."

"Oh yeah, there's been some doozies!" he concurred. "Many years ago in New Jersey, a body-building couple picked me up. They were on their way home from a Mr. & Mrs. Jersey Shore competition. Judging by the trophies I had to squeeze in next to in the back seat, they must have done quite well. Both wore tank tops…of course. After I got comfortable, I stared at them. I actually became quite alarmed at the size of their trapezius and deltoid muscles…her's especially. I had this strange foreboding: what if she should overpower me and steal my wallet? What if the incident appeared on the evening news? *Twenty Year Old Hitchhiker Brutally Beaten and Robbed by Female Bodybuilder...***Oh, the Horror!***"

"Once we got to talking however, I gradually felt more at ease, although the guy's body was quite disconcerting as well. He was so thoroughly depilated. That and his shiny bald head gave him the look of an overgrown fetus on steroids, something you might read about in a supermarket tabloid: *Enormous Fetus Terrorizes Downtown Los Angeles. Residents Urged to Keep Doors Locked!* Of course I kept all those thoughts to myself."

"I did ask them a question however, to sort of break the ice." I asked, 'How much can you guys clean and jerk?'"

"The young lady turned half way around, hung her well- defined arm over the back of her seat...I fought off a curious urge to touch it... and she corrected me. 'I think you're confusing us with power-lifters. We're body builders.'"

"Of course I immediately apologized. Then I discovered some common ground when I steered the conversation to Arnold Schwarzenegger—the bodybuilder, before he became governor. The conversation flowed quite smoothly from that point on until they dropped me off somewhere in Staten Island."

The drive continued and so did the conversation. They learned more and more about one another. As planned, they also shared the driving. Usually after every pit stop, or after refueling, the other person took the wheel.

Will even paid Annie a compliment, "You know... you're a pretty good driver!"

"... for a woman, you mean?"

"Did I say that?" he smiled. Will realized how his seemingly well-intentioned remark might be misconstrued, so he attempted to wriggle his way out by way of another story, of which he had more than a few.

"It's just that I feel comfortable as a passenger," Will defended, "and I can't always say that's true. I remember one time back in college I hitched a ride with a guy who turned out to be this incredibly erratic driver. For no reason at all, he was constantly giving it the gas and then letting off... seventy miles an hour... down to fifty...back up to seventy...down again to fifty...all within a mile or so of driving. It drove me crazy. I'd never gotten car sick, but I was starting to feel a bit woozy, so I asked do you mind if I drive."

He got real angry. "'What...you don't like the way I drive?' I said it wasn't that, it's just that I was starting to feel a little...light-headed."

"So he jams on the brakes, pulls over to the side of the New York Thruway and yells, 'Get the fuck out of my car, you ungrateful bastard!'"

"Oh my God," said Annie, "What happened then?"

"What could, I do? I grabbed my backpack and got out."

"Did someone else pick you up?"

"Well, you can get into real trouble trying to hitch a ride alongside the New York Thruway, so I decided to walk to the next service area which was over ten miles away, but it turns out that even walking alongside that road is illegal. Sure enough, a state trooper picks me up."

"Then what happened?"

"I told him what happened with the erratic driver. He was sympathetic, and generously offered to drive me down to the next service station. "Maybe you can get a lift down there... but just don't be sticking your thumb out when I'm around, because technically, I can't allow that, but I can't do anything about something I don't see,' he winked, 'if you get my drift.'"

"So he drops me off and says good luck, and I discreetly position myself near the entrance ramp to try and hitch a ride. A few minutes later, who should be exiting the service area? Non other than my friend the erratic driver. He must have stopped for gas or whatever and was now getting back on the highway."

"What did you do?

"I changed from thumb to middle finger and proceed to give him the most theatrical bird you have ever seen!"

Will's depiction of that encounter forced a laugh from Annie. "Then what did he do"?

"Nothing. What could he do? But it was a terrific catharsis for me! Anyway, a few minutes later, I did get picked up. This guy wound up taking me all the way to my destination... minus the herky- jerky"

"Was that the only time you ever got kicked out of a car?"

"Actually, it wasn't. It happened on another occasion. Do you want to hear about it?"

"Of course…you're not going to leave me hanging?"

"So on this other occasion, I happened to be out West in the desert somewhere between Tucson and Tucumcari…"

"Wait… I know that song… 'Willin'…or is it 'Weed, Whites and Wine'…Little Feat… back in the seventies…"

"Yeah, but this is not a song," Will reminded Annie. "It's a true story. You asked if there was another time I got kicked out of a car, and I'm going to tell you about it."

"Sorry…I won't interrupt again," she uttered, feigning apology.

"As I was saying, I was somewhere on a desert highway between Tucson and Tucumcari on a terribly hot day, the kind of day you could fry an egg on the pavement. I wasn't having much luck hitching, mainly because there was only about one car every half hour passing by. I was standing in the shade of what seemed to be the only tree in the county, and it wasn't providing much relief at all, but better than nothing, when an old Lincoln Continental appeared in the distance, shimmering in the heat like those mirages you see in Clint Eastwood Westerns. I was desperate. So instead of just sticking my thumb out, I put my hands together as if praying and practically stood in the middle of the road. The fellow pulled over and said, 'Hop in. Name's Uriel.'"

"I thanked him immediately and complimented him on his car. People like to hear that. Uriel was probably in his fifties and resembled that fellow in the painting, *American Gothic* —the one by Grant Wood— high forehead and pursed lips. Of course he didn't have the pitchfork in his hand, but if he had, I wouldn't have been at all surprised. Turns out he's a bible salesman. His trunk was filled with several hundred bibles, King James Version, no surprise. Different prices I was informed, depending upon whether it was leather bound, or the words of Jesus were printed in red, and so on. 'A bible for every budget', he proclaimed."

"Then he starts to speak with great fervor and says, 'I bring the Good News right into people's homes. I've got the best job in the world. My brother used to sell vacuum cleaners door to door, and we would always have this debate over who had the better job. I would remind him that people say cleanliness is NEXT to Godliness, and not the other way around!'"

Then he lowered his voice. "And from a practical standpoint, having the weight of all those bibles in the trunk of my car helped me drive in the snow. That's when I lived up in Minnesota. Notice how the rear end of my car is so low? Books weigh a lot you know. Back in Minnesota, my wife would occasionally borrow my car, but one day she says to me, 'I won't drive that car anymore unless you take those bibles out of the trunk, Uriel!'

I said, 'Why is that, Ethel?'"

"She says, 'cause folks are always telling me, 'Ethel, your rear-end is sagging!'"

Uriel paused a few seconds before repeating, "Do ya get it...your- rear-end- is sagging?"

"I laughed, of course," said Will. "I mean, the guy had been nice enough to pick me up."

"Folks up in Minnesota got that weird sense of humor!", chuckled the Bible salesman. "That's where I'm originally from, Minnesota. Thirty years ago, my father advised me to come down here, it's better for the arthritis he said. He still lives here. We just celebrated his hundredth birthday."

"A hundred years old," I said, "that's incredible!"

"Yeah, but he doesn't drive at night any more."

"???!"

"So about a half hour into our travels," continued Will, "we're going through some real desolate country with only an occasional roadrunner scampering across the highway and maybe a sidewinder or two. Uriel was doing most of the talking, mainly about religion. I found out that he was on his way home to tend to his flock. It took awhile to realize that he wasn't talking about sheep, but about his small congregation. He was also a preacher for a little church somewhere in the Sanger de Christo range in New Mexico, but bible sales were his main income. The name, Uriel, comes from the book of Isaiah, I learned."

At any rate, soon enough Uriel asked, 'By the way, what religion are you'?"

"Now had I had more time to think it over, I certainly would have come up with a better answer than the one I gave him. But what I said was, 'Uriel, I currently profess belief to no organized religion, and consider myself…. Agnostic'".

"That response hung in the air for a moment. A pained expression crept across Uriel's face. He then gripped the steering wheel so hard, his knuckles turned white, and he slammed the brakes. I had to brace myself against the dashboard with my hands, since 1964 Lincoln Continentals didn't have seatbelts. Before even come to a stop, Uriel screamed, 'Get out of my car and rot in hell, you, you….**atheist!**' With that, he literally pushed me out the door and took off like he's driving a hot rod Lincoln."

"I bounce off the pavement, but quickly recovered. At the top of my lungs, I yelled, '**That's NOT what Jesus would do.. you..hypocritical.. UN-CHRISTIAN!!**' all the while watching that old Lincoln roar down the highway. I admit it was not the most clever riposte. I didn't have time for much better. Then I limped out into the middle of the road, cursing and giving him the finger, non of which he probably saw or heard."

A minute or so later, I just stepped off the highway, shoulders slumped, realizing that I would soon die. I was in the middle of a desert. There was no shade to be found. I raised my shirt to form sort of an awning and estimated that I could survive maybe a half hour. If I remained calm."

"Maybe twenty minutes later, I heard the sound of an engine in the distance. Shielding my eyes, I squinted to see what was coming. Lo and behold, racing back toward me was the old Lincoln and Uriel. *Now I'm fucked* I said to myself. He's probably going to finish me off in his righteous rage. *These guys all carry guns.* There's not a witness for miles. He'll leave my body for the vultures that are already soaring above my head as if they knew something. So I resign myself to my fate, thinking a bullet between the eyes was better than heat stroke."

So here comes Uriel speeding back to me. He makes another abrupt U-turn, comes screeching to a halt and the passenger door swings open. Instead of killing me like in some Cormac McCarthy novel, he says in a perfectly serene voice, 'You were right, Will. That is *NOT* what Jesus would have done. Please come back into the car. I need for you to forgive me.'"

"You're kidding, right?" I yelled.

"Calm as could be, he replies, 'No, I am not *kidding*. I am asking you to please get back in the car and forgive me. I heard what you yelled about being…**Un-Christian…**and as I drove down the highway, either it was a voice from God, or maybe my own conscience speaking, I can't be sure… but anyhow, something said: *Uriel, that young man was right. What you did was **Un-Christian!*** The next thing I knew, something was applying pressure on the brakes and turning the steering wheel. I found myself driving back to you, knowing what it was I had to do. I am asking you to come back in the car and forgive me!" He even added, "I seek absolution from you, Will!"

"'Absolution'…can you imagine? Maybe he threw that in to add some biblical gravitas to the situation," Will reflected.

"Well, of course, I did get back in that car with Uriel, still imploring me to forgive him, and I kept insisting that all was forgiven, and he kept asking me are you sure, and me having to reassure him that I was never so sure in all my life. This went on for a while, when out of nowhere he asks, 'Are you still sure you don't believe in God?'"

"…???. Then it dawned on me. That son of a bitch Uriel did that whole thing, kicking me out of the car and leaving me to die out in the desert and then coming back to pick me up, to try and put the fear of God into me …to get me to believe in God! Maybe to make me think I had just experienced some sort of a miracle. We were out in the desert after all, isn't that where most of those miracles took place?"

"Really a pretty clever if not somewhat fiendish game plan he came up with. But I didn't confront him or let on in any way that I knew what his little scheme was. I just let him do most of the talking. Every time he said he was sorry and would ask for forgiveness, I told him that I forgave him, but more importantly, Jesus had also."

"About an hour later we came into a little ranching community on the Arizona – New Mexico border. I saw a sketchy looking motel, and suggested to Uriel that this would be a good place to drop me off. That I needed to get a little rest and that place looked fine…it even had a swimming pool."

"Uriel pulled over, and I said thanks, safe trip."

"Then he says, "Say Will... would you be interested in a bible? I can take something off the price.'"

"Can you imagine that: **Would you be interested in a bible? I can take something off the price?** I thought for less than a second and said no thanks, that when I check into my room, I would surely find a Gideon's Bible, like Rocky Racoon did."

"'God bless you' said Uriel, and drove off."

Annie looked at Will in all earnest, and with a truly mischievous smile said "But you never answered my question."

"What question was that, Annie?"

"I asked if you thought I was really a good driver, or just a good driver...*for a girl?*"

When they stopped laughing, Will checked the time. "Annie, let me ask you something. Are we still going to drive straight through, or are we going to find some place where we can lay our heads?"

The *I'll sleep while you drive* plan hadn't quite worked out as planned, what with all their conversing, and they were both getting a bit tired.

"I wouldn't mind a hotel," agreed Annie, "as long as we split the cost... meaning I don't want you picking up the tab."

"It's a deal then."

So just like that, the original plan (call it "Plan A"), driving straight to Austin, taking turns behind the wheel while the other slept, was happily scrapped for a "Plan B".

They continued driving down the highway for a while, when Annie asked out of the blue, "By the way, I'm just curious. When did it first occur to you that we might be spending the night together?" She looked at Will with a little smile.

"Let's see," thought Will. "What time was it this morning when you took pity on me and picked me up?"

"It was eight o'clock in the morning. I know that because I had just checked the clock while getting on the entrance ramp."

"Then the possibility of spending the night together occurred to me at approximately... eight...O...One!"

CHAPTER 8

ITS A TOPSY-
TURVY WORLD

—cᴧɔ—

"You sure you're up for this?" asked Annie.

They would be getting a late start the following morning. *For all the right reasons* thought Annie who was still delightfully sore when they awakened.

"We're in Texas, Annie. You are now the tour guide," replied Will.

After crossing the Sabine River and entering Texas, Will and Annie had consulted the map. They decided to get off I-10 to bypass Houston and continue on state highways. A strategy that wouldn't save time but would allow them to mingle with folks on Main Street, USA. Maybe find the "soul of America".

Their destination was a small liberal arts school between Houston and Austin, Howard Zinn College. Annie had already informed Will that it was considered to be the most liberal institution of higher learning in Texas, Will countered that the term "liberal-Texas-College" was an oxymoron.

"And that's exactly why I'm taking you there: to dispel those preconceptions folks from the East have. I think you'll be pleasantly surprised. Besides, there's some great little cafes in town. This weekend there's a shindig called "Topsy-Turvy Days", lots of activities to promote what they call 'Strength in Diversity'. Consciousness-raising stuff. Like I said, they're super liberal."

"How do you know about this?"

"It was on TV while you were in the shower."

"Sounds like fun…let's do it. Maybe we'll get to see some of those bluebonnets on the way."

"For that, we're a few months too late. They usually bloom in April."

"Too bad! But let's do something Texas on the way. You have any Willie Nelson CDs?"

"It would be sacrilege for a Texas girl not to!"

"So put on some Willie. What's your favorite? Wait, don't tell me. Each time we ask that question, we seem to come up with the same answer. How do we know we're not trying to prove something, like how much we have in common?"

"OK then, pull over to side of the road."

"What for?"

"Just pull over."

Will pulled over and came to a stop. Annie handed him a small note pad and pen. "Now write down your favorite Willie Nelson song and don't let me see what you wrote. Then I'll do the same, and we'll compare answers. No cheating!"

"Cheating…?"

"You know what I mean. No looking!"

They each wrote something on their scraps of paper, then folded the pieces.

"Shall I do the honors?" offered Annie.

"By all means, it was your idea."

As she began to unfold the scraps, Will requested, "Drum roll, please!" And in theatrical MC fashion. "…and the answer iiiis?"

Annie hammed it up a bit herself looking back and forth at the scraps, dragging out the drama. "Sheet number one says '**Angel Flying Too Close to the Ground**' and the other one says…(long pause)…(shouting)…'**Angel Flying Too Close to the Grouuuund!**'"

"Jeez, you've got good taste in music!", congratulated Will. "C'mon, let's go …I'm getting hungry!"

And off they went with Willie on the stereo, "If you had not fallen… then I would not have found you…"

The main drag of the little town was quintessential East Texas. A central mall with footpaths and enormous old live oaks festooned with Spanish Moss ran down the entire length. On both sides, small boutiques, head-shops, sporting equipment and bike shops, book stores and a nice selection of cafes and bars beckoned. Strung across Main Street were several large banners announcing: **Welcome to Topsy-Turvy Days!** Four of the central blocks were closed to vehicles for the weekend. Will and Annie found a parking lot, put Walter on a leash and ambled into town.

Much of what they saw was theater. Students, faculty and members of the community were involved in various skits or performance art in which they acted out typical American street scenes, but with a twist. A band from the music department provided further entertainment. At the moment, a scrawny young man with a wispy beard was performing a passable cover of Bob Dylan's "Blowin' in the Wind."

First stop was a tavern featuring a creative taco lunch special. Will enjoyed bars. He felt at home in both dive bars or the more intellectual establishments, and would even tweak his vocabulary as circumstances required. For example, he knew better than to use terms like "taciturn" or "verisimilitude" in certain milieus where they might not even know what a "milieu" was. Over the years, he had developed two separate vocabularies: one for the sophisticated crowd and a more basic argot for blue collar emporiums. The way some piano players seamlessly switch from boogie-woogie to Chopin.

He peeked through the window and saw a waitress carrying her order to a table. "Is the place dog friendly?", he inquired.

"As long as you got a friendly dog it is!", replied the waitress.

Will looked at Annie, "That would be Walter!"

They walked in and sat at the bar. After Walter sniffed around, he curled up at the foot of Annie's barstool. They place orders. Annie, the iced tea, Will a local craft beer. On TV was a boxing match featuring a white boy and an African-American, neither familiar to Will.

A young man who appeared to be a student had taken a stool within conversation range. "Who you rootin' for?" he asked.

"Joe Palooka," answered Will. "The guy in the blue shorts...not that I actually know anything about either of them."

"Why you rooting for him then? Asked the young man. "I'm just wondering if maybe you picked Palooka just because he's white?"

It was at this point that Will picked up on the young interlocutor's line of inquiry. He decided to play along. "Actually, not 'maybe'," responded Will. "In the absence of any information about two boxers, I usually pick the white guy."

There was a brief pause before the young man accused, "I'll bet you don't think of yourself a racist, but you certainly sound like one!"

A long time ago, Will had been given advice about how to successfully win a debate or argument: the one asking the questions controls the discussion. So he decided to go on the offensive, so to speak, by asking a few questions of his own. "Let me ask you a question then. Do you ever watch any international competition, like World Cup Soccer, the Olympics or Grand Slam Tennis?"

"Of course..."

"So let's say Americans are competing against the Russians, or for that matter, any foreigners like the Spanish or Germans. Who do you root for?" asked Will.

"The Americans, of course. We always root for the home team!"

"OK," continued Will. Now let's say you actually do know something about the athletes. For example, let's say it's a pain-in-the-ass-whiner like McEnroe or Connors...you may be too young to remember those guys, but trust me...and the opponent is a class-act like Roger Federer... not that they ever played against one another...but just for arguments sake. Do you still cheer for the American?"

"Probably yes... he's still American."

"You say 'yes, he's still American'. So your identification as an American is so strong you'd be willing to overlook character defects..."

"It's not the same thing," the young man countered.

"It's not the same? I think it is. Just like you root for an American because you are American, for the same reason, I, as a white guy would probably root for the white guy, assuming I have no personal information about either athlete that would compel me not to."

Choosing a momentary lull in the conversation, Annie nudged Will, reminding him that his tacos were served five minutes ago, and were getting cold. Walter has perked up, and now sat drooling and probably perplexed as to how humans can have food placed in front of them and not immediately devour it. Will picked up his taco, took a bite and chased it down with the lager.

"No, it's not the same thing!" came a renewed challenge from his young adversary, a few decibels higher.

A concerned look came over Annie's face. Walter's also.

"You can't choose your race...you're born that way. It's not the same as nationality!"

"Really? When did you choose to be Americano ?"

"Actually choose? OK. Maybe I didn't choose...but I was born American!"

"So maybe the best you can say," reasoned Will, "is that after reciting the pledge a few thousand times in school, and singing 'Oh say can you see...' at sporting events, and seeing that being an American is actually not such a bad gig, you chose to REMAIN an American?"

"It's still not the same as race. You don't choose to be black or white and you certainly can't change your race!"

"Really? You can't change your race? What about Michael Jackson? Will paused. "That was a joke by the way... but while I'm at it, I have another question. Do you think most African-Americans are rooting for the white guy in a boxing match?"

"Probably not."

"Of course not. They're more likely to root for the black guy simply for the simple reason that they themselves are black...and that's OK. You wouldn't call them 'racist' for that!"

"OK, you may be right, but it's still not the same thing. I can't explain it, but it's not!"

"Look," said Will, a bit more conciliatory. "I'm not passing judgement on the whole thing, but personally I see nothing 'racist' about rooting for an athlete with whom you happen to share the same race or ethnicity. Just like there's nothing wrong with rooting for the Americans in the Olympics. I do the same thing…it's a matter of whom you identify with. Let me give you another 'for- instance'."

"Go ahead."

"Are you familiar with with the so-called 'Battle of the Sexes' tennis match, the one between Bobby Riggs and Billy Jean King?"

"I wasn't born yet, but I know the match you're talking about."

"Alright, you know the match. So who would you have rooted for back then?"

"Probably Billy Jean King." A pause followed before the young man asked, "So what are you going to tell me now, that I identify more with females than males?"

The young man got off his barstool and stood over Will. Up until now, Will hadn't realized how big the guy was.

A look of real concern came over Annie's face. She had heard of barroom brawls but had never actually witnessed one, despite living in Texas all her life.

Will handled the young man's insinuation calmly. "Of course not," he said. There are many reasons why one might identify with or cheer on a certain athlete."

Red-faced and still hovering over Will, the young man demanded, "And what would another reason be?"

"Because the athlete could be the 'underdog'," answered Will. "It may have nothing to do with nationality, sex or race or stuff like that. You look like the kind of person who always roots for the underdog— and I think that's an admirable quality by the way—it shows you have compassion. Would you say I'm right?" *As long as you ask the questions, you control the discussion.*

"Come to think of it, you're right." A smile formed across the young man's face. "I do always root for the underdog."

"I thought so!" Will concluded. "Let me buy you a beer."

No one felt more relieved than Annie. She was certain that she was about to witness her first barroom brawl and wasn't sure how she would have handled that or how it might upset Walter.

Will then joined his former adversary now turned best-friend in a beer. The young man's name was Ethan and soon they were all having a grand old time. Ethan and Annie graduated from the same high school in Austin, something they discovered five minutes into the conversation. He even knew Annie's younger brother! Who doesn't love a small-world story?

Just before Annie and Will...and Walter...were about to continue their stroll through the rest of the Topsy-Turvy Days festivities, Ethan said quietly, "Look, before you leave, I have to tell you guys something."

"What's that Ethan?"

"This whole thing, the boxing match on TV and me confronting your 'racism', it was a set-up."

"A set-up?" asked Will, "What do you mean 'set-up'?"

"The boxing match?" Ethan confessed. "It's on a loop. Come back in an hour or even two hours and you'll see the same match. I'm a psych major. We came up with this strategy to engage folks about their beliefs regarding other races, people with different religions and sexual orientations. By using various contrivances, like the black boxer vs white boxer film loop, we hoped to get folks to honestly confront their prejudices."

"Wouldn't it have been just as easy to tell folks that they're about to watch a situation on TV that may evoke certain feelings having to with racial or sexual bias, and then engage them in discussion?" Will offered.

"We talked about that," Ethan explained, "but felt that if people knew what they were getting into beforehand, they may not respond honestly. Kind of like *I know what you're trying to get me to say so I'll just be politically correct.* By the way, I also apologize for accusing you of saying that I identify more with women. I responded emotionally. We were trained to remain nonjudgmental, and not allow our own feelings and opinions to get in the way."

Will assured Ethan that he didn't take it personally. Ethan confided that he and his fellow psych majors had rehearsed all possible scenarios that would come out of the "Boxing Match", but confessed that he wasn't quite ready for the arguments that Will raised.

"Maybe I should have prepared more," he lamented.

"No problem," Will assured Ethan. "By the way, I think I owe you a beer, so next time we bump into one another it's on me."

Once again, Will and Annie excused themselves. As they exited, Will turned and said, "Good luck. What you're doing here is a good thing. Folks need to examine their beliefs. Then Will pause a moment before asking, "By the way, who actually wins that boxing match?" That got a laugh, always a good way to part company.

Will and Annie continued down the main drag to take in more of the activities. Within a minute, they came upon a scene, quite provocative, featuring a group of baby carriages with black babies pushed by white nannies.

"When do you ever see that?" asked Will.

"Exactly," replied Annie. "It's a topsy-turvy world today."

Shortly after the baby carriage brigade, they came upon a "fashion show". It featured male models wearing outrageously provocative outfits and strutting down the cat-walk with that exaggerated gait that female models do. Some of the men wore dresses exposing their chests or accentuating their buttocks. A few wore signs that read "professional sex-objects", not that it was necessary. The panel of female judges made comments like, "Nice butt! Show us some thigh!" Or yell, "More cleavage, honey!" Hilariously, the male models complied.

"Now that was funny," said Will.

"It's supposed to raise consciousness about the pervasive sexism in the fashion industry,", Annie reminded.

Will looked at the audience. Mostly women. None were laughing.

They continued their stroll. All around them were guys on bicycles carrying take-out orders. Delivery guys, white, delivering to Blacks and Central-Americans. Topsy-turvy.

The performances were well choreographed and done in the manner of film loops repeated over and over. The next skit they came upon featured two well-dressed, middle-aged African-American men walking down a sidewalk. Five young white males strode toward them. Off to the side stood two musicians. When they crashed cymbals, the black men quickly grasped for their wallets. No explanation needed!

Another vignette was being performed throughout the day, on the hour. Will and Annie arrived just in time. A considerable crowd had already gathered. It began with sirens blasting and two African-American "policemen" exiting a "police car". Guns drawn, they approach a white teenager "hiding" something behind his back.

"Stop where you are and show us your hands!" demanded one of the cops. The youth hesitates. **"I said show us you hands!"** repeats the officer, louder. Slowly, the youth pulls a half-eaten banana out from behind his back. Within seconds, the young man is blown away in a hail of 'bullets'. The "victim" performed his role in melodramatic 1950s Western fashion, jerking violently then clutching on to a nearby stop sign. It took ten or fifteen seconds for him to finally slump to the pavement. There was a slight technical glitch with the fake blood, but when it eventually came spurting, you could hear the oohs and aahs.

Walter became upset and barked, but Annie bent down, whispered in his ear, and whatever she said, it soothed him. He just stood there panting. It was turning into a tough day for Walter.

A short while later they walked into a small auditorium in which a panel discussion had just begun. The panelists included three clergymen (a rabbi, a pastor from the local AME congregation and a Unitarian minister), a sociology professor, the president of the campus Gender Studies Club and the college's director of admissions.

The moderator was announced as a black studies major, but he was a young white guy with dreadlocks that kept falling out from beneath one of those floppy knit hats worn by Rastafarians. He wore Birkenstocks and a Bob Marley t-shirt with an ornate Marijuana Leaf. He was doing an admirable job keeping the discussion focused and getting audience involvement.

"This should be interesting, let's stay," suggested Annie. She and Will took seats near the stage with Walter once again lying at their feet.

The panelists were providing meaningful insights. Audience questions were being handled quite well. The discussion concerned matters of racial profiling. It was evident that the demographics of attendees leaned toward highly educated and liberal. The entire room was in *simpatico* to the cause.

Will decided to contribute to the talk. Annie sat at his side, but as the point he was trying to make started to become clear, she became concerned. *Here we go again.*

Will began. "So here's the thing. Could it be that young black men are more likely to be arrested for violent crimes, both justly and unjustly, and be convicted of those crimes, both justly and unjustly, as well as actually be more likely to commit those violent crimes? Not necessarily crimes against white people, but crimes against other black people as well? And yes," he added, "also more likely to be victims of not only racial profiling, but profiling based on age and sex, as well?"

The rabbi asked Will to clarify his remarks. Some of the other panelists and the young moderator began to show concern…as did Annie. Walter, lying at their feet was probably the only one in attendance that remained indifferent.

Will thought for a moment, then continued…*As long as you ask the questions, you control the discussion.*

"OK." He turned around and looked at the audience.Then he raised another question. "Who is more likely to commit a crime…correction…a crime of violence… a male or female?"

He paused to look around him. The room was silent. "C'mon folks! Let's not be so fearful of committing some 'politically incorrect *faux pas*… the answer should be based on statistical realities!"

A voice in the back finally volunteered, "It's probably going to be a guy… but what's that got to do…"

"Thank you," said Will, cutting him off. "The gentleman said 'probably a guy'. Not just 'probably'. It's a statistical certainty: Men commit more violent crimes than women. Imagine that! Did we just make some sort of sociological breakthrough?" *Be careful with the sarcasm…back off…*he warned himself.

"Next question: who is more likely to commit a violent crime? A young man or an older man?" Once again, Will looked about trying to engage audience members. This time a female voice responded rather immediately and was joined by others. Of course the consensus was that young men were more likely to commit such crimes.

Will went on. "So if I said to you that a young person, male gender, is more likely to commit a crime… again, we're talking violent crime…than an older woman, am I guilty of ageism or sexism, or am I simply stating a statistical reality?" A low murmur went through the audience.

"Alright, final question." He looked around and waited for conversation to subside. "Who is more likely to commit a violent crime? A black person or white person?" No one dared answer. Will waited, then provided the answer that no one dared utter. "OK then. I'll tell you the answer. An answer supported by statistics gathered state-by- state. Blacks, specifically young black males are more likely to commit violent crimes than whites. And if you take it a step further, statistically, whites are more likely than Asians to commit violent crimes!"

"Yeah, but older people and females are not more likely to be unjustly charged or convicted of crime. Nor are they being profiled," yelled an older white lady in the back of the auditorium. Her comment started a minor uproar.

Will had almost sat down but stood back up to respond. "You're absolutely correct. I think where racism really enters the picture is when you look at the culpability of whites in fostering the systemic racism that leads to high violent crime rates among blacks…."

Although he had raised his voice, much of what he had said could not be heard. Either the room had gotten too loud or folks had simply heard enough from him. Or maybe because they were still outraged by something he said earlier: *Blacks commit more violent crimes!*

A chubby guy in his forties, wearing khakis and an Izod shirt, stood up and yelled at Will, "Who the hell do you think you are? And who the hell invited you here anyway?" The woman beside him, probably his wife, was making an effort to physically restrain him.

The partisan crowd cheered the man. Someone yelled, "You tell him, Earl!"

Will stood up and looked at Mr. Izod. Waving a piece of paper at him, he yelled back, "You invited me here! It's right here in your flyer: Topsy-Turvy Days are open to the public! We invite…actually it reads, '**You are urged to attend!**'"

Then the chubby fellow named Earl got red in the face and screamed, **"Well in that case, we uuuuurge you to get the hell out of here!"**

Laughter broke out and so did a chant that quickly gained momentum: "Earl!... Earl!...Earl!...Earl!...Earl!...Earl!

Things were going rapidly downhill.

The young moderator stood at the edge of the stage, microphone in hand, dreadlocks shaking. "People! People! People!" he implored. His Rastacap had fallen off and was picked up by the Unitarian minister. The clergyman didn't quite know what to do with it but briefly held it to his nose, intrigued by the not unpleasant, funky cannabis fragrance.

And then Walter began to show signs of upset. Dogs don't relish pandemonium. Annie tried desperately to calm Walter down, but kneeling down whispering in his ear wasn't working. The poor dog had been through so much today, and now this.

Will was especially concerned for Annie. Not just that the angry crowd might do her bodily harm, although that might still be possible, but that they would verbally abuse her for having anything to do with a loser such as himself. Guilt by association. He looked around. He saw faces distorted by anger, even women's faces. That especially concerned him. Women, he knew, could be cruel. Especially when it came to other women.

Annie held Walter's leash in one hand, grabbed Will by the other, and in no time at all, they were out the door. With rapid strides, they headed back to the parking lot. Annie kept looking over her shoulder as did Will, who said, "If I see that Earl character, I'm going to…"

"…Oh no you won't!" interrupted Annie. "We're getting into the car and driving to Austin! We're lucky if we don't get tarred and feathered and rode out on a rail!"

"They still do that in Texas?" quipped Will.

"Not as much as they used to…."

CHAPTER 9

MEET THE PARENTS

Upon arrival at the car, Walter jumped into the backseat, Annie into the passenger seat and Will slid behind the wheel. They skedaddled out of town at NASCAR speed. Once they hit the main highway, Annie suggested slowing down a bit. There was no posse on their tail.

Ten minutes later, her pulse rate back to normal, Annie asked, "Will, have you ever gotten yourself into trouble before for being…maybe a bit too outspoken?"

He mulled the question over for a few seconds. "You mean is this the first time? No, maybe not the first time," he admitted, rather sheepishly.

"How did I know that?" Then Annie turned and looked at him. She put her left hand on the back of his neck and massaged him gently. "Maybe your comments during that panel discussion could have been more… filtered?

"Filtered?"

"Just a little, maybe?" Annie nudged. "You know, when you engage in polemics, which is what you were doing, you have to expect some backlash."

"Annie, didn't their own flyer say 'Topsy-Turvy Days provides a forum to discuss critical issues freely in an open and non-judgmental environment' or something close to that?"

"It did," agreed Annie, "but they may have had something else in mind…"

"…Yeah, like speak freely as long as you spout the part line. As long as you don't cross *their* boundaries!"

"Look, Will. I was in agreement with most of what you said back there, and I certainly support your right to say what you did…but…I don't know…maybe you were misunderstood." Annie paused, then added, "The moderator could have been more in control. Maybe he was too young to be handed that responsibility."

Will attempted to steer the discussion in another direction. "Was that funny when the young fellow's Rasta hat fell off?"

"Even funnier was when the minister picked it up and sniffed it. Did you catch the look on his face?"

The recollection of that scene brought on an uncontrollable fit of laughter. Laughter in the form of release from the terrifying episode from which they had just emerged—relatively unscathed. If what they say about laughter being the best medicine is true, they were getting what they needed.

When Annie finally recovered, she reminded Will, "Before we get too far, I need to call mom. She wanted to make a nice dinner for us, and needs a heads-up on when we expect to arrive."

Will could hear Annie's end of the phone conversation, and so could pretty much piece together what her mom was saying. At one point, Annie placed her hand over the phone and looked at Will. "Mom wants to know if there's any foods you don't particularly like."

"Tell her I have the Will Rogers approach to food."

"Will Rogers?"

"Yeah. I never met a food I didn't like!"

"Oh, she's going to love you…Mom was born in Oklahoma you know, and Rogers is one of their notable native sons."

"I'm already scoring points, am I?"

Following the phone call, they got back on the highway. Annie slipped Willie Nelson back into the CD player, and by coincidence, "On the Road Again" came on. She turned up the volume, and soon they were both singing along, feeling the serendipity.

Another fifteen minutes or so later, Annie turned down the volume. "Look Will, just so we're on the same page here: I did NOT pick you up hitchhiking! My parents know I can be somewhat of a free spirit, but..."

"I get it, I get it! So let's come up with an acceptable story and hope neither of our noses grow when we tell them how we just happened to wind up in the same car for the last couple of days."

"I already told them we met at the conference, at a cocktail party my company sponsored, and that I volunteered to drive you as far as Austin. I also told them I'd be taking you to the airport tomorrow so you can continue on to Missoula." Annie paused before throwing in "...and that we had separate rooms last night..."

"So I take it your parents already know a little bit about me."

"Of course. You don't think I'm just going to show up with some total stranger, do you?"

"Then share with me everything else you told them, and then let's plug up any gaps so we get the story straight. And how come I'm starting to feel like a teenager?"

A few hours later, they pulled into the driveway. Annie's mother, Laura, was already outside the door waiting. Walter jumped out of the car, ran up to her and gave her an exuberant face-licking-tail-wagging greeting. Laura reciprocated with an affectionate hug, then turned her attention to Annie. "I missed you honey! How did the conference go?"

"Missed you more, Mom! The conference went well. I'll tell you all about it. But first I want you to meet my travel companion."

Laura thought to herself, "*'Travel companion'? He seems to be more than just that.*"

Will thought to himself, "*'Travel companion'? Is that all I am is a 'travel companion'?*"

Annie thought to herself, "*Did I just call Will my 'travel companion'?*"

Will reached his hand out. "I finally get to meet Mrs. Arnold..."

"I'll have none of that, Will!" she quickly corrected him. "It's Laura! Unless of course you want me to address you as 'Mr. Kraft' for the rest of your visit!"

"Leave your things in the car," Laura suggested, "We'll get to it later. You must be exhausted. Come inside and relax for a while. How was that Topsy-Turvy thing at Zinn?"

Annie didn't give Will a chance to respond, just in case he was thinking about it, "Great, Mom. They really put a lot of work into it. We had a wonderful time, didn't we, Will?"

Before entering the house, a beautifully maintained Arts and Crafts bungalow from the 1920s, Will stepped back for a better look. "I love your home! I've always been an admirer of this architecture."

The Arnolds had been in Austin since the late sixties. After earning his doctorate in biology, Tom was hired as an adjunct at the University of Texas. Within a few years he received tenure as a full-time professor. A few years later his wife Laura also joined the faculty as a professor of English literature. Shortly after, they bought the house in which they have lived ever since.

Laura never tired of telling people about this first venture into home ownership. "You should have seen this house thirty years ago when we bought it," she shared with Will. "Real Tobacco Road. It had been on the market for over a year. Nobody would touch it. For Tom and me, it was really the only thing we could afford. We looked beyond its dilapidated condition and saw potential—and thirty years later, we're still here."

"I still remember when we first pulled up to the place in our old Buick Roadmaster (at the mention of the vehicle, Annie smiled at Will and gave him a wink). Annie, who was five at the time, was with us. When we stepped inside to look it over, she called it the 'tumbly-house' because she thought it was going to fall down."

"I did call it that," confirmed Annie. "For a long time, I was certain that the 'big, bad wolf' would come by and blow the place down!"

When he entered the home, Will was immediately struck by the interior décor. It spoke volumes about the family's taste: sophisticated and understated. He also noticed the beautifully set dining room table. *Do these people eat like this every evening?* He wondered.

The artwork hanging above the sideboard then caught Will's attention. He walked over to get a closer look at three beautifully framed photographs of Native Americans. "Are those Edward Curtis photos?" *Was his sense of wonderment too obvious?*

"Tom got those about thirty years ago, right after we almost finished renovating the house. I say 'almost' because it seems that a house is never truly *finished*, if you know what I mean. Anyway, he knows a lot more about them, so I'll let him tell you. Do you know how few people recognize those images?"

"Speaking of Tom," said Laura, "I'll let him know that you're here." She called out, "Tom, we've got company!"

"Just a second…" came a deep voice from the next room.

"He's not being rude," Laura whispered to Will. "He'll be out just as soon as Jeopardy is over." Looking up at the clock, she added "which should be in less than a minute."

From the TV room came the sound of the Jeopardy theme music, and Tom's voice victoriously announcing "What is kleptoparisitism!" and then, "Be right out, hon!"

In another few seconds they could hear a conciliatory Alex Trebek informing the contestants, "Nooo…I'm afraid you're you are all incorrect. The answer is 'kleptoparisitism"…when eagles *steal* fish from ospreys is an example. The reason, by the way, that Benjamin Franklin promoted the turkey as our national bird…"

"Yes!" shouted Tom as he entered the room.

"That always gets him excited," explained Annie, "when he gets the answer to Final Jeopardy, and none of the contestants do."

Tom stepped toward Will and shook his hand. "So you're the fellow that's going backpacking in Montana for a week. Wish I was going with you!" Next he gave his daughter a hug. "How'd the presentation go? Did you get a standing ovation?"

Seeing Annie becoming embarrassed by the "Daddy's-little-girl" treatment, Laura intervened. "OK, dinner's ready. Why don't you guys get seated and Annie and I will serve."

Will had been in the house for less than a half hour. The filial piety was obvious, but not surprising. Annie had already told him a great deal about her parents. She had wryly described her father as being an "only-child", even though he was number four in a family of eight boys and girls. When Will asked how that could be, Annie provided an ornithological analogy. "My aunts and uncles joke that if they had all been birds, Tom would have been the robust demanding one that pushes the others out of the nest! As a youngster, even many of his teachers mistook him for an 'only-child'."

The description of her father caused Will to wonder if such a larger-than-life figure hadn't given Annie unattainable expectations of men.

Laura then barked a loud command from the kitchen. "Jake! Dinner's ready...and we've got company!"

"Now you get to meet my kid brother," warned Annie. "Get ready!" It was said with affection.

Jake bounded down from the second floor in that gangly, two-step-at-a-time manner of teenage boys and made a bee-line for the dining room table. An aura of invincibility enveloped him. "My *little* sister is back!" he announced, emphasizing their size difference with a hand gesture. After giving Annie a generous hug, he turned to Will.

"I'm Jake!" he said, extending his hand.

"Pleasure to meet you, Jake. Your sister's told me a lot about you! Will Kraft."

Annie and Laura soon appeared at the table with platters of food. There were now six at the table, if you counted Walter, who had strategically positioned himself at Tom's feet. This had been his spot for years, forever hopeful that some delicacy would fall off the table. On occasion the strategy was rewarded.

"Serve yourselves," Laura invited. "Jake, save some for the rest of us please. I hope you like stuffed cabbage, Will. Annie told me you had... what did she call it? Oh yes, 'the Will Rogers approach to food.' I like that! I'm originally from Oklahoma you know, or did she already tell you that? Tom and I met while studying at the University of Illinois."

There was quiet while everyone filled their plates. Following his first bite, Will's palate immediately took note of the delightful expression of caraway and raisins in the stuffed cabbage. He turned to Annie's mother, "This is outstanding, Laura!"

Annie rolled her eyes at his shameless brown nosing. *This is outstanding, Laura!* She said nothing, of course, but would certainly bring the matter up to Will later. In private.

"Well in that case," Annie's mother acknowledged, "my labors in the kitchen have been more than rewarded by your gusto inn the dining room. It's an old recipe from the Bohemian side of the family…Halupki."

Will was quick to raise his glass. "Well in that case then, here's to the Halupki family…"

The words were barely out of his mouth, when the entire Arnold family burst out in laughter, Jake himself snorting out wine and practically falling off his chair. Even Walter seemed to be in on the joke, now standing up, tail wagging.

Will thought, *Did I just miss my own punch line?*

Being the first to recover from laughing, Jake explained. "Will, *Halupki* isn't a family name! It's what they call stuffed cabbage in Bohemian!"

Jake's explanation then caused Will to laugh, triggering another round of hilarity. Tom then added, "Heck, for so-called 'Bohemians', those Novaks weren't Bohemian at all! Laura's folks were such prudes… real fuddy-duddies!"

"But at least they could make decent Halupki!" retaliated Laura. "Your mom couldn't defrost a TV dinner!"

"Grandma Novak ran a heck of a kitchen," Tom conceded. "I'll give you that."

Over the course of dinner, conversation flowed smoothly. Maybe the 'Halupki" comment had broken the ice, though Will didn't thin so. He never detected any 'ice' to begin with. They were just a fun, easy-going family. Will could see where Annie got her sense of humor from.

Tom expressed delight in the fact that Will took such an interest in the Curtis photos, and proceeded to share the story of how he acquired them. They were from a colleague at the University. The colleague had hoped to pass them along to his daughter and son-in-law, Tom explained, but they had a home filled with Abstract Expressionist art, and neither expressed any interest in "those Indian pictures."

Annie switched the discussion to her brother, Jake, who along with everyone else was enjoying a glass of wine, though his allotment was considerably less than the adults. Looking at Will, she said, "Jake picked out he wine. He fancies himself an oenophile, and plans to become a world-famous sommelier or maybe a professional wine critic. Quite a lofty goal for someone who won't be served alcohol legally for another three years…"

"…in the United States, that is!" Jake reminded Annie.

"…which is where we happen to live," rebutted the sister.

"Maybe I'll move to Europe then, where you can drink at sixteen. Last year my French teacher took a bunch of us to France during spring break where I was introduced to wine culture…"

"…and Juliette!" Annie chimed in, reminding him of his little fling.

Laura quickly took sides and reprimanded her daughter. "You're embarrassing Jake…stop it right now!"

Tom suppressed a laugh. Will smiled. Laura's stern demeanor shifted, and now she too smiled. She got up from her seat to put her arm on Jake's shoulder in a show of support.

Unfazed, Jake continued. "So anyway, in addition to Gothic architecture and stuff, I started to learn a lot about wines on that trip. But the wine that accompanies tonight's dinner is a 2001 Kuhlman Cellars Zinfandel from the nearby Hill Country. I thought it would pair well with our main course. Most people don't know anything about Texas wines!"

Annie couldn't resist bringing up a recent episode. "A month ago, we had guests over for dinner, and Jake was our sommelier." She turned to her brother and asked, "Do you want to tell this story, Jake, or should I?"

"Go ahead, Annie. You think it's so funny."

"OK then. So Jake was our sommelier, giving us all a little clinic on how to properly taste wine by swirling it around in your mouth and so on. 'Tell us what flavors you are experiencing,' he instructed.

One of the guests, Mom's friend Betsy, says she detected hints of plum, cherry, a slight amount of licorice… and Dawn Dishwasher Detergent!"

Everyone at the table laughed, including Laura. Her's a more sympathetic laugh, but that wasn't necessary since Jake himself was laughing the hardest.

Annie continued. "Dad, you bailed Jake out by quoting Goethe… what was it you said?"

On cue, Tom responded, "'By seeking and blundering we learn' --- Johann Wolfgang von Goethe."

Will attempted to re-engage Jake in a more serious discussion regarding his career goals. "Jake, how's a boy from Texas going to succeed in such a competitive and sophisticated milieu? I understand the Somm test is quite tough."

Jake was aware of the challenge ahead of him. "Study real hard for the test! Since I'm starting young, I'll have a head start. Then once I pass, I hope to use my 'humble' Texas origins to my advantage. Folks in France may be intrigued by the notion of a sommelier from Texas. "Imagine that," they'll say. "He's from Texas, he knows wine and he speaks perfect French! You never know with the French. I heard that old American comedian, Jerry Lewis, was huge over there!"

Again, much laughter.

A second bottle of Kuhlman's came out, and the repartee became even more animated. Dinner ended with a perfect homemade pecan pie on which Will lavished great praise and was promptly offered seconds. To add to his appreciation, Laura provided a piece of apparently factual information that legally it can only be called "Texas Pecan Pie" if it's made from Texas pecans. That was the law.

"I have no reason to doubt that," Will assured Laura.

It was almost midnight when Laura looked up at the clock and pointed out the time, and didn't Annie have to take Will to the airport tomorrow morning?

Annie escorted Will to the guest bedroom and gave him brief instructions on how to cope with the bathroom plumbing's idiosyncrasies. Certain that her parents were already in bed, and that Jake was downstairs watching TV, Annie kissed Will goodnight which started with a peck on the cheek...

CHAPTER 10

ON THE ROAD AGAIN

Will and Annie awakened early the following morning. Will wanted to get an early start so he wouldn't be late for his *flight to Missoula* which is the story he and Annie had agreed upon, far more palatable to Tom and Laura than Will's hitchhiking plans. The parents probably had more than a few questions concerning the provenance of this so-called *travel companion* their daughter just showed up with out-of-the-blue. But they all seemed to have hit it off quite well.

Laura once again gave a virtuoso kitchen performance by baking a batch of poppy seed *kolaches*, another page out of her Bohemian recipe book. Will gladly accepted a second cup of coffee and then another half cup. He knew he wasn't going to get coffee this good at the truck stops of the American West.

After farewells to Tom, Laura and Walter (Jake was still asleep...), Will and Annie climbed into the Buick. At the northern edge of Austin, Annie pulled over on the entrance ramp to I-35. Will thought this was cool being that the PBS program, "Austin City Limits" had always been one of his favorites. He had already prepared a sign, *"Dallas, please!"* The "please" being Annie's idea

She showed some concern by asking, "Do you want me to stay with you until you get picked up? What if you don't get a ride?"

"Not a great idea," said Will. "They might think we're Bonnie and Clyde."

"OK then you crazy bastard," Annie smiled, "good luck!"

Will had never heard a curse come out of Annie's mouth, and under the present circumstances, saw it as an act of tenderness.

"And I will be expecting a phone call tonight!" she demanded. Her eyes began welling up with tears.

They embraced and kissed. Will felt the warmth of Annie's tears against his cheeks, but said nothing. After what seemed like forever but still not long enough, Annie let go, made an about face, got into her car and sped off. Will watched through his own watery eyes as the car disappeared into the distance.

After regaining composure, Will focused on the task at hand. For the moment he was brimming with optimism. Austin was a liberal oasis and one of his pet theories was that liberals are more likely to pick up hitchhikers. Especially those who never left that magical era, *the Sixties.*

But after ten minutes and dozens of vehicles passing by, his optimism began to waver. At that moment, a Volvo station wagon, a young lady behind the wheel with a little boy in the back seat, pulled over. *Goes to show you never can tell.* She opened up the back for Will to toss in his gear.

As Will slid into the passenger seat, the youngster greeted him with, "You're not a serial killer, are you?"

"That's Dawson, my four year old. I'm Betty, his crazy mother. We're on a road trip looking for America — like Simon and Garfunkel. In the interests of full disclosure, I should also tell you that I'm a journalist on assignment. Anything you say might appear in my piece."

"Hi, Betty, I'm Will."

"Nice to meet you, Will."

"So a few days ago, Dawson heard 'serial killer' on the evening news. I know he thinks it's C-E-R-E-A-L because he asked me why anyone would want to kill a box of Cheerios," Betty chuckled. "Anyway, as I was pulling over to pick you up, I asked, 'Dawson, he doesn't look like a *cereal killer,* does he?'"

They both laughed. Will got a kick out of that little vignette, and soon shared some of the funny things that had come out of his own children's mouths over the years. Betty turned out to be as witty as one would expect from a writer, and the drive was filled with delightful anecdotes.

Dropping Will off at an exit somewhat north of where she was planning to get off, Betty said, "It's really not that far out of my way, but I know the area quite well, and I think your chances of getting a ride here are better than back where I would normally get off."

"That is a true gesture of kindness," said Will. The thought occurred to him that she must have done a bit of hitchhiking back in her younger days. *People who hitchhike are more likely to pick up hitchhikers.* It turned out that Betty had good instincts. He had barely finished writing "Oklahoma City" on his sign when a fellow in a big Mack Truck, minus the trailer, pulled over.

"I'm Hawk," said the driver as Will climbed aboard. "It's Henry Hawksbill, But everyone calls me 'Hawk'... except for my folks. Where you goin' to in Oklahoma City?"

Will turned to answer and saw that Hawk was Native American, and the contour of his nose may have had as much to do with his nickname as did the surname. His face seemed to have jumped out of a portfolio of Edward Curtis photographs.

"Well, the truth is I'm on my way to Montana. Missoula, actually. I'm Will, by the way, Will Kraft," reaching over to shake hands.

"Good thing you were truthful, Mr. Kraft... always best to be truthful, because I'm delivering this rig up to a fellah in Wichita. I don't know how you're planning to get to Missoula, but here would be my advice: continue north on I-135 from Wichita to Salina where it ends, and then pick up I-70 all the way to Denver. From Denver, go north on I-25 through Wyoming until it intersects with I-90. From there it's a straight shot to Missoula."

"That's pretty much what I had in mind, Hawk."

Will and the driver carried on a spirited conversation from that point on, mostly about all things Indian: differences between tribes, life on the rez and so on. Will learned that Hawk was full-blood, Cheyenne on his father's side, Choctaw on mom's.

They had been traveling for about an hour or so, when Hawk turned and looked at Will rather seriously. "Will, what do you know about the 'Trail of Tears'?"

Will paused for a moment. He did know something about this dark chapter in American History, but as a white man felt strangely awkward discussing it with a Native American. Was it a case of "collective guilt"?

71

He paused for a few seconds, did a quick risk assessment and decided to try and answer.

"The Trail of Tears," he began hesitatingly. "Please correct me if I'm wrong, but that took place back in the early 1800s when President Andrew Jackson evicted the Cherokee people from their ancestral homelands in the East and ordered them on a forced march to so-called 'Indian Territory' in Oklahoma."

Will continued, providing as much information as he knew. Hawk, listening patiently, would occasionally supplement Will's story with additional facts.

When Will finished, Hawk took over.

"You got a good grasp on the story. Actually, you know a hell of a lot more than any white man I've ever met. Yes, it was Andrew Jackson…that no-good bastard…pardon my French…who was behind legislation known as the Indian Removal Act Of 1830. And it wasn't just the Cherokee."

Hawk explained that the tribes removed were called the so-called "Civilized Tribes", because they had adopted the white man's ways. He spoke at length, providing much detail about this atrocity. Hawk called it 'ethnic cleansing'. Will had never before heard that term used in the context of American History.

There was a lull in the conversation before Hawk started again. "And you know what really galls me? Getting visibly upset. "White folks have this expression 'Indian-giver' for folks who give something away and then take it back. **'Indian-giver!'** This coming from people who broke just about every treaty ever made with the Indian—over and over again—promising land, then taking it back!"

Another uncomfortable lull in the conversation followed, which was fortunately broken by Hawk. "Jeez, I don't know about you, Will, but I am awfully hungry. You like steak? I know a great place a few miles north of here. Let me buy you a steak dinner!"

"What? You buy me dinner? You don't have to do that…"

"You're right. I don't HAVE to do that… I WANT to do it! Do you know that you're the only white guy I ever met that knew anything about the Trail of Tears?"

"But I didn't…"

"...and I don't care how much you know or don't know. You know more than the others! Don't argue with me...I'm buying!"

Over dinner the conversation continued, but mostly about other things and not so much Indians. When dinner was finished, Hawk asked, "One for the Road?" The men moved to the bar, where the bartender served up two Lone Stars. Hawk handed him a hundred dollar bill. "Take everything out of here... and both dinners, too."

The bartender rang them up at the register. He returned with a twenty, a ten and a five and some singles. Hawk picked up the twenty- dollar bill and stared at it for a few seconds before uttering, "Andrew Jackson, you bastard!" Then he called the bartender back. "Could you break this twenty for me?"

"Sure. What d'ya want...tens...fives...singles?" asked the bartender.

"Doesn't matter...doesn't matter! Just break the damn **twenty**!"

CHAPTER 11

THE PROMISE

—◦⟊⟊◦—

Will and Hawk climbed back into the big rig. Hawk turned the engine over, put it in gear and soon they were back on I-35 heading toward Wichita. The sun was beginning to set, and the western sky took on a bright crimson color. All in all, thought Will, he had made good progress in the twelve hours since leaving Austin. His thoughts turned to his soon-to-be ex-wife, Katie, and a feeling of despair took over. Not wishing a the bad karma to take over, he was relieved when Hawk addressed a more practical matter: finding a place for Will to spend the night.

"I know an inexpensive motel up near the I-70 interchange," Hawk suggested. It's family owned, and because it's a bit far from the highway, they keep the prices down. Maybe if you mention my name, they'll give you a break. But then again, maybe not…no promises."

A half hour later, they pulled into the parking lot of a small, twenty unit motel. The "No" on the neon No Vacancy sign was not lit. Hawk pulled his rig up to the office and shut down the engine. He then reached under his seat, pulled out a small plastic bag and placed it on his lap.

"Will, I'm wondering if you can do me a little favor. If you can't, or would rather not, I understand. It's no big deal."

Will was hoping that in some small way he might be able to repay Hawk for his generosity at the restaurant. "Go ahead," he said, "talk to me."

"I told you earlier that I was Cheyenne on my father's side."

"I recall."

"Well my great-great- grandfather on that side of the family actually fought in the Battle of Little Big Horn. According to family lore, he killed at least two cavalrymen that day, the day that Custer made a serious error in judgement. Then again, there's a fine line between courage and stupidity. Did You know that Yellow Hair had his horse shot out from under him eleven times during combat? Maybe his luck just ran out."

"At any rate, like many Indians that day, my ancestor participated in the frenzy that followed the battle, probably the mutilations as well, although most of us Indians do not speak of this today. Those acts have to be judged in their historical context, as an outlet for the rage that Indians must have felt for the atrocities and humiliations they suffered at the hands of the white man over the years."

"The glory of that victory over the U.S. Cavalry was short-lived. The Indians scattered into small groups, some fleeing to Canada. But with the great Bison herds nearly wiped out, and with little to eat, most of my people were skeletal-like when they were rounded up by the army and placed on reservations."

"But in the aftermath of the battle, my great, great grandfather took a small collection of brass buttons and stripes from an army uniform. Those vestiges of that final Indian victory— if it could be called a victory— the brass buttons and uniform stripes, remained hidden by my family and were passed along from generation to generation. My father recently handed them to me." Hawk held up the bag for Will to see.

"Which brings us to the present," inferred Will.

"Exactly," continued Hawk. "For the past several years I've been having a recurring dream. The first time I had this dream, I quickly wrote it down when I woke up, which it turns out wasn't necessary, since the dream kept coming back anyway. In this dream, I am walking on a path toward a valley in the distance, a valley that is post-card beautiful. I can make out flowing streams, flowering trees and herds of elk and buffalo grazing in the meadows. I can even smell the fragrances and hear birds singing."

"As I get closer, I can make out a white man approaching the valley from the opposite direction. But any time we look into each other's eyes, the valley recedes further into the distance. I decide the only way to get into the valley is to avoid looking at the white man. And sure enough, by doing this, I am able to get closer and closer. The valley is so beautiful, that I start to run toward it."

"But once again, I can't help myself. I make eye contact with the white man. And once again, we move apart from one another and further from the valley. You know how frustrating dreams can be. I become more and more upset at my inability to enter that valley of abundance. *Surely the white man and I could share it's bounty,* I think to myself. So disturbing is the dream, that I usually force myself to wake up."

"I've had this dream so often I had to ask myself what it all meant. We Indians place great significance in dreams and their meanings, and soon the meaning became obvious."

"I realized that the dream comes from the anger within me," reflected Hawk. "More than anger, darkness. You saw it earlier when I was I was telling you about Andrew Jackson and the Trail of Tears. I still won't carry twenty- dollar bills. That I cannot do. I know there are some —even my own people—that think I'm crazy for that, but I have to take a stand somewhere. I've already joined a group of indigenous people petitioning to remove Andrew Jackson from our currency. It would be easy to replace him. How about Red Cloud? Or Crazy Horse?"

"I don't know if reconciliation between Indians and white people will ever be possible—complete reconciliation that is. But I don't want those dark feelings controlling me."

"Maybe reconciliation begins with one heart at a time. I know that the change in my own heart won't happen overnight, but I can take certain steps to get there. Maybe you can help me."

Hawk then handed the bag to Will. "In this bag are the brass buttons and corporal stripes my great-great- grandfather took that day at The Battle of Little Big Horn. Go ahead. Take a look at them."

Will removed each item from the bag and examined them closely. For a few minutes, not a word passed between the two men.

After this long pause, Hawk resumed talking. There was a slight tremor in his voice. "When you head west on I-90, you will be going right by the battle site. If you could, Will, I'd like you to bury these items into that sacred soil. You'll have to do it in secret. The park rangers wouldn't be happy if they found out what you were doing." He chuckled at that last remark before becoming serious again.

"I'm asking you to do this for me because I know I won't be able to get out there for many years." Hawk then spoke with greater conviction. "It needs to be done, Will."

Will wanted to answer Hawk, but could not find the right words. Hawk sensed what he thought was reticence. He began to regret placing Will in this awkward situation, so he opened the cab door and said, "Tell you what. I'm going inside to talk with Pete the owner. See what I can do about getting you a deal on a room. You sit here and think about what I'm asking of you. No pressure—and I mean that. If you can't do it or for whatever reason are unwilling to, you don't have to explain. Just say so. I'll understand."

Hawk got out of the cab, walked to the office and stepped inside. Will remained in the cab and thought about Hawk's request. He knew what he had to tell his friend, even if it was going to be difficult.

When Hawk got back a few minutes later, Will didn't wait to be asked. "I made my decision," he declared. "I *will* bury those items for you...I give you my word!"

Hawk placed his hand on Will's shoulder and lowered his head. For a minute or so, although it felt longer for Will, the men sat in silence. Finally, they got out of the cab. Hawk then walked around to Will. They shook hands and embraced.

"I want to hear from you, Will," Hawk insisted. "Be careful!"

Will picked up his belongings and his hiking stick, and walked toward the office. He turned around for a final wave as Hawk slowly pulled out of the parking area.

Upon entering the motel office, he was greeted by a handsome, middle-aged man with distinctive Native-American features. "Mr. Kraft ? Here's your key. Room 18... our luxury suite!" Then with a wink, he added, "Only kidding... but it is clean."

"I'm sure it'll be fine. How much?"

"For you? Nothing. It's already been paid for."

CHAPTER 12

THE PROPHET

The following morning Will woke up completely rested. Setting the alarm clock turned out to be unnecessary. He was already in the shower when it went off. He got dressed, grabbed his backpack, small suitcase and hiking stick, then walked the short distance to the motel office to drop off the room key.

Pete, the proprietor, welcomed him.

"C'mon in! Did you sleep well? I hope so…that's a brand new mattress in that room."

"No problem sleeping, I'm happy to report."

"Good! Then have a seat over there," pointing to a small couch, "and I'll get

you your breakfast. How do you like your coffee?"

The offer caught Will by surprise. "I had no idea breakfast was included!"

"It's not. You can thank your friend, Hawk. He saw to that. When you're ready, I'll drive you back to the interstate."

"Wow, breakfast and chauffeur service…"

"Unless you'd rather walk," said Pete. "It's only eight miles!"

"Eight miles! It didn't seem that far last night. I think I'll take you up on your offer."

Will had already made up the sign "Salina/ I-70...Please!" It was roughly ninety miles to Salina, a modest distance by the standards of the American West. Although the morning was still a bit nippy, temperatures were supposed to reach the mid eighties later on, with bright sunshine. All in all, a great travel day.

Pete dropped Will off at the northbound entrance ramp. Will took time to position himself strategically, and then assumed a proper hitchhiking posture: upright, not too close to the roadbed, confident demeanor, without brashness and a slight affect of humility. Each part of the country required a slightly different style, those subtle nuances discernible only to hitchhikers who take their craft seriously. Will could always fine tune that demeanor.

He wasn't keeping a tally, but probably twenty or so vehicles passed by in the next fifteen minutes. Always interesting, Will thought, how different each driver was. Some never make eye-contact, keeping a fixed stare at a vanishing point ahead. Some look at you sympathetically, even apologetically, but don't slow down in the least. Others view you with pity...or was it scorn?

It was probably the twenty fifth car that finally pulled over...a young man in an old Pontiac with a sun-baked patina and rusty bumpers. Will slid into the passenger side and immediately paid a compliment: "Nice Pontiac...Catalina?" *To make sure things got off to a good start*

"Very perceptive!" The young man affirmed. "You know your Pontiacs, my friend. It is indeed a '62 Catalina, my grandfather's pride and joy. She actually sat in the garage for fifteen years after he passed. Then I resurrected it. I'm talking about the car...its name is Lazarus."

After sitting for a minute or so, Will got a better look at his chauffeur. A pleasant looking young man in his mid to late twenties, he sported a full beard and long hair. His garb consisted of a full-length brown robe patched in spots with burlap. In the back seat were stacks of cardboard boxes and pamphlets. The fellow's long hiking stick took up most of the car's width. It got Will's attention.

"Nice stick you got back there...I'm sort of an *aficionado*. What kind of wood?"

"Hickory," the young man replied, "and your's?"

"Sassafras."

"Quite nice also," acknowledged the driver. "By the way, you can credit your stick for me picking you up. I saw you standing there sort of biblical-like and said to myself that anyone who takes that kind of pride in his staff…well that just speaks volumes about that person. I'm sure your 'staff comforts you'?" quoting Psalms 23.

Will played right along. "Now that you mention it, 'it doth indeed comfort me'!"

"So what would be your purpose up in Salina, my wayfaring stranger?"

The young man pronounced it 'Sal-eye-nah'. Will took note because that is definitely not how he would have pronounced it.

"Actually, I plan to get on I-70 and head west, destination Montana. So if you can get me anywhere close, it would be appreciated."

"I can get you up to I-70, but from there I head east to Topeka and Kansas City."

"I-70 would be great," replied Will appreciatively. Making conversation, Will asked, "So what do you do?"

"I'm a prophet."

"A prophet? I didn't think that was much of a career path these days."

"There's not as many of us as there used to be," replied the young man quite seriously.

Will couldn't let this one get away. "Are you a prophet of subway halls or tenement walls?"

"…Suburban Malls," he replied without hesitation. "I warn about the dangers of materialism and the superficiality of consumerism: the false prophets. For example, I have an entire sermon on footwear that I deliver in front of shoe stores."

"I never introduced myself. I'm Will Kraft. And you are…?"

"Mahatma O'Neil"

"But what if a person really needs a pair of shoes, Mahatma? Say he has holes in his soles or is barefooted?"

"Good question, Will. I actually deliver that shoe store talk barefooted, even though it's said to be against the law…which it really isn't. The title of that talk? 'Is there a Hole in Your Soul?'…that's S-O-U-L, so there's this double-meaning. I have another talk I give in front of shirt stores. That one has the title, 'Would You Give Me the Shirt Off Your Back?'"

"You must get a lot of shit from store owners!"

"I certainly hope so," Mahatma laughed, "All good prophets are persecuted!"

"By the way," Will asked, "Have you ever heard that song, 'I Love my Shirt' by Donovan? It's from the sixties."

"Can't say that I have."

"Check it out," said Will. "I think you'll love it!"

Will and Mahatma O'Neil carried on their lively discussion all the way to Intersection of I-70 near Salina, Kansas, which Will now knew was pronounced "Sal-eye'-nah".

CHAPTER 13

AMBER WAVES OF GRAIN

———— ∿ ————

Standing alongside the entrance ramp to I-70, Will exuded confidence. Finally he would be heading due west, destination Montana. Only one large city, Denver, stood in the way, but he was already looking past Denver to Missoula. From past travels, he knew that in this small Montana city he would find great outdoor supply shops where he could purchase freeze-dried food and sundry items for his backpacking adventure.

Missoula was also home to the University of Montana and the opportunity for cultural experiences. The Montana Museum Of Arts and Culture was a must. Their collection of Western Art always put him in the mood for his wilderness explorations. The Monty Dolack Art Gallery downtown was also a favorite. The artist's whimsical take on wildlife always put a smile on Will's face. His daydreams made it feel close, but he had to remind himself that Missoula was still 1300 miles away.

What to write on the sign? Would **"Denver, please"** appear presumptuous? On the other hand, weren't travel distances relative? Back in his home state of New York, requesting a hundred mile lift would seem impertinent. In America's heartland, however, it's a rather modest swath of roadway. In a perfect world, a motorist would shortly pull over and cheerfully announce, "Heck, I'm on my way to Missoula...hop in!" Will knew that the world was far from perfect.

At the risk of offending the many fine and upstanding citizens of America's heartland and its annex in eastern Colorado, there's not a whole lot going on in this part of our country, unless "spacious skies and amber waves of grain" is your thing. Fortunately, Will got picked up often enough to make some good progress.

Two military guys, one a cadet at the Air Force Academy and the other an Army officer stationed at Fort Riley, Kansas, got Will a few latitude degrees further westward.

Then a group of six "twenty somethings" from Topeka pulled over. "Hop in, dude!" Will managed to squeeze into the back of the van. They were on their way to see Dave Matthews at the Red Rocks Amphitheater. They were all having a good old time. Maybe too good. If they had gotten pulled over by highway patrol, it would have looked like a scene from a Cheech and Chong movie. The pipe was passed to him more than once, but Will decided the vehicle's ambient air made that unnecessary, and did he really need to add a marijuana bust to his list of woes?

The speakers were right behind his ears and the volume a bit beyond his comfort zone, but Pink Floyd's "Us and Them" certainly created a mood as did Eberhard Weber's "Colours Of Chloe". The concert-goers would have been more than willing to take Will all the way to Denver. "Dude," they urged, "we could definitely score a ticket once we get to Red Rocks!"

Will wisely requested to get dropped off at an exit near the eastern border of Colorado.

Upon exiting the van, he found himself in the High Plains community of Burlington, Colorado. Only an hour or so of daylight remained and Will knew it was best to confine his hitching to daylight hours, so he got himself a room in a modest hotel just off the interstate. After checking in, he realized that he had crossed into the Mountain Time Zone, which also explained the early setting of the Sun.

Taking the motel manager's advice, Will had dinner at the local VFW. The food was pretty much what he expected, but the enthusiasm with which patrons ate was somewhat contagious and served to remind him that taste is such an individual matter, *De gustibus non est disputandum*. Some folks were giving him the he's-not-from-around-these-parts look, so Will made an effort to not leave any scraps on the plate lest they feel slighted.

He took a few beers back to the room and made some phone calls. First to Katie and the boys. His wife answered but quickly handed the phone to his oldest son, Eric. They chatted awhile before the phone was passed to Paul. During his conversation with his children, Will mentioned that he had met a genuine American Indian. The boys asked their father if he wore a headdress with feathers. At the moment Will admitted, he was only wearing a John Deere cap. Most likely, their dad explained, he saved the feathers for special occasions and holidays, but definitely not on Columbus Day!

After about ten minutes, Will requested, "OK boys, I'll call again… could you please put mom back on the phone?"

He heard Eric yell loudly, "Mom…Mom! Daddy wants to talk with you!" A muffled ten second delay followed before Eric got back on the phone. "Mom is not feeling well…maybe call back tomorrow."

Will took a deep breath, and instructed, "Be good…and tell Paul to be good also…and no fighting with one another!"

Ten minutes later he called his parents in Florida. His father picked up. "Dad, I'm in Colorado. Eastern part. Not in the mountains yet. I expected to be in Missoula by now, but…it's a long story. Anyway, how's everything by you?"

"Good Will…actually very good. Bruno called today about your car. The transmission got delivered sooner than he expected. So the car should be ready in a few more days. Do you want me to pick it up?"

"Good idea, Dad. Tell me how much I owe you and I'll send a check. Jeez, if I had known it was going to be fixed so soon, I would've planned things differently."

"You know," his dad responded sympathetically, "he always does that, Bruno does. Tells folks the car won't be ready for whatever number of days, then calls and tells them it's fixed much sooner than he thought. I think so customers won't always be pestering him, 'Hey, Bruno, Is my car ready yet?' Then when the car is finished sooner than expected, they're all thankful. 'Oh, Bruno, you're the best, Bruno!'"

"At any rate, he also said the engine problem was nothing serious. It's fixed and he told me the car should be good for another 300,000 miles. I said, Bruno, would you back that up with a written warranty? He said, 'Mr. Kraft, you have a good sense of humor!'"

Ernie continued with his son. "Will, your mom is at a neighbor, so let me ask you something. You said you're in Colorado. Do you think you do me a favor and see if you can't get me John Denver's autograph? You know Mom's such a fan, and she's got a big birthday coming up."

"John Denver's dead, Dad! Remember that plane crash..."

"I know that!" Ernie shot back, annoyed. "But I thought that maybe there would be some memorabilia around, like a signed album cover or something. Kind of like if you go to Memphis, I'm sure you can get Elvis stuff."

"I'll try, Dad. But it may not be as easy as it is with Elvis."

"How's that?"

"Think about it. Do you see John Denver impersonators all over the place?"

The third phone call was to Annie. Will gave her a progress report and told her about some of the colorful characters he met, like Mahatma O'Neill and Hawk. He also shared with Annie the promise he made to bury some artifacts at Little Big Horn and the whole story behind that. Annie told him to be careful, that it was probably a federal offense.

"Where exactly are you calling from," she asked.

"From the geographical center of Nowhere," he replied, "Burlington. Colorado. Did you ever eat at a VFW hall?"

"I hear they have a great wine list," laughed Annie.

Annie caught Will up on what's been going on in her life and mentioned that her parents had been pestering her a lot since he left about her so-called *travel companion*. Even her younger brother was in on the act which she said she kind of deserved for all those years she tormented him.

They spent over an hour on the phone. Right before the conversation ended, Annie asked, "When will I see you again?"

Will assured her that he would make that happen as soon as possible.

After he hung up, John Denver's "Annie's Song" entered his thoughts and would not leave— the annoying "ear-worm" —*You fill up my senses, like a night in the forest.*

CHAPTER 14

KEEPING THE PROMISE

Will was up early the following day. So far, the "early-bird- gets-the-worm" strategy had been paying off, and being an early riser for most of his life, why stop now? He was hoping to make it as close to the Battle of Little Big Horn National Monument as possible by the end of the day. Sheridan, Wyoming specifically. It was a rather ambitious goal considering that the driving time would be almost eight hours. Actual time depended upon so many variables, chief among them engaging the sympathy of approaching motorists. His sign read, "Denver...Please!" Annie's simple suggestion of adding "please" seemed to be working.

Will's first ride was a young man wearing jeans and a flannel shirt who himself had a back pack in the rear seat. A kindred spirit thought Will. A Black Lab sitting in the passenger seat dutifully jumped into the backseat when Will opened the passenger door. The Toyota Prius was plastered with peace signs and logos of environmental organizations: The Sierra Club, Audubon Society and one that read, "My other car is a bicycle".

Will immediately complimented the young man on his commitment to the environment. "You already drive an eco-friendly car, and by picking me up, just cut your carbon footprint in half!" He had always felt strongly about the environmental ethos of hitchhiking and did not hesitate to point it out at every opportunity.

Will actually made it all the way to Sheridan, Wyoming by the end of the day even though it meant arriving at 9PM. The six hundred mile, fourteen and a half hour trip required four separate rides. He shared the driving with the last fellow. What actually happened was that the chap first passed him by, then fifty yards later came to a stop, followed by backup lights, always a welcome sight to seasoned hitchhikers. It meant that he had done an appraisal and reached a favorable conclusion. The driver backed up, rolled down the window and asked...no, begged, "Would you mind doing some of the driving? I'm starting to nod-out behind the wheel." Will had just hit the hitchhiking jackpot!

"No problem... no problem at all," replied Will. The fellow immediately got into the passenger seat and Will got behind the wheel. Perfunctory introductions were made, and within five minutes his driver-turned-passenger was fast asleep. Will lowered volume of the radio and picked up the speed to a steady eighty five. Being in Wyoming, he was still being regularly passed by mostly everybody.

I-25 ran into I-90 which pretty much paralleled the Rocky Mountain Front. As evening approached, a reddening glow began to silhouette the Bighorn Mountain range, becoming increasingly alluring as they approached Sheridan. It was 9PM when they pulled into a motel parking lot on the city's south side, Will still behind the wheel. He had been on the road for over fourteen hours, and his rides had taken him nearly six hundred miles. *Not a bad days work*, thought Will.

Once in his room, he spoke on the phone with Annie for about a half an hour. Five minutes after his head hit the pillow, he was fast asleep.

Early the next day, Will stood on the northbound entrance ramp to I-90. A young couple in their twenties pulled over about ten minutes later. The sign "Little Bighorn Battle Site" left no room for the customary "please!" but immediately attracted the couple's attention.

In a mildly accented English, the woman said, "We see your sign. We are also visiting the battlefield. Come join us please...Martin and Iris Wetzel from Stuttgart, Germany."

For this trip it was a first. Not the fact that Germans picked him up, but that the very first car of the day did. He took it as a good omen...he'd have been a fool not to.

Martin informed Will that he and his wife had landed the previous day at Denver International, and today was the first full day of their tour of the West. They both spoke excellent English. After exchanging greetings, Will shared his plans to eventually get to Missoula and then go backpacking into a wilderness area near Glacier National Park.

"I thought you were going off on an adventure," exclaimed Iris triumphantly. "Not everyone carries a backpack and a *Wanderstock* (hiking stick)! I even said to my husband that perhaps you were off on a 'vision quest'."

"Wow, *vision quest*... I hadn't thought about it in those terms, but in a way that is exactly what I am doing." He spoke slowly and enunciated carefully so the Germans would understand. "When you are alone in the wilderness with your thoughts, a certain re-wiring of the brain (...he pointed to his head) does in fact take place. I am hoping to bring greater clarity to my life, so in some sense, it will be a certain spiritual experience. Maybe a vision of some sort will come to me." Will paused before asking, "By the way, how do you know what a 'vision quest' is?"

"We Germans have always had a deep fascination with Native-American culture," volunteered Martin. "Have you ever heard the term 'Indianthusiasm'? Sometimes it's called 'Indiantumelei'. They are pretty much... how do you say...synonymous? They translate to 'Indian enthusiasm'. Such enthusiasm for things Indian has existed in Germany for centuries."

"Have you heard of the author, Karl May?" asked Iris. "In the late 1800s and early 1900s, he became one of Germany's most successful writers. His subject matter had always to do with the Wild West and Indians. A fictional Apache named 'Winnetou' appears in many of his stories."

"Yes," added Martin. "Another character is Winnetou's German blood-brother, 'Old Shatterhand'. He could knock a man silly with one punch. Winnetou and Old Shatterhand formed a bond similar to the Lone Ranger and Tonto. In fact, many people think that pair may have been based on Karl May's characters. The most interesting thing? Karl May himself first visited America well after he wrote all his stories, and even then, never got further West than Buffalo, New York!"

"Some believe that May's popularity explains why so many Germans have this fascination with Native-Americans" Iris continued. "Of course it could be the other way around, that because we had the fascination to begin with, his books became so popular. How you say in America... which came first, the chicken or the egg?"

"So that's why you're visiting America," asked Will, "to learn more about Indians?"

"Pretty much," answered Martin. "By the way, is it still OK to use the word 'Indians'?"

"Depends upon whom you ask," said Will. "Even Indians or Native-Americans...or First-Nation People are divided on that issue. Whenever I'm with a Native-American I ask first. You can't go wrong if you refer to them by tribal affiliation... Cheyenne, Sioux or Crow."

Martin and Iris had a meticulously planned itinerary. They would be traveling through the West visiting as many battle-sites as possible, such as Little Bighorn and The Battle of the Rosebud and several more. Some pow wows were also on the agenda such as the one up in Heart Butte, Montana.

"Funny, in Germany we would be getting dressed up in our finest Native-American costumes, but we were advised not to do this here in America. Would that be...*verboten*...forbidden?"

"It wouldn't be against the law or anything, but it would probably not be a good idea. Are you familiar with the term 'cultural appropriation'?" asked Will.

"Yes," answered Iris. "We have a term for it as well...'*Kulturelle Aneignung*.'"

Will then shared the experience that he had with Hawk a few days ago. He told them the story in all it's detail, including Hawk's disdain for twenty dollar bills because of Andrew Jackson's image. Then he showed them the plastic bag with the cavalry uniform items, and told them about the request to bury them at Little Big Horn in order to restore peace to Hawk's soul. Martin and Iris examined the brass buttons and uniform stripes with great interest.

Martin then expressed concern. "Will they permit you to place these things in the ground? Would it not be *verboten*...against the law?"

"I'm sure it is against the law," replied Will. "I'll be very careful."

"Maybe we can help you then," volunteered Iris. "What if Martin and I stood ...*beobachten*...what is the English word..."

"Stand lookout," Martin interjected. "What if we watched over you so that you will not be ...captured...caught, I mean?"

"You would do that? I don't want you guys to get into trouble!"

90

"How would they know what we are doing?" Martin reassured Will. "We will stand apart from you and give you signals…Indian signals. Did you know that Native-Americans, especially the Plains Tribes had a very elaborate type of '*Zeichensprache*'…how do you say this word?" Martin then made some hand gestures.

"Sign language" Will said.

"That is the term, yes… 'sign language'. Then Iris showed Will some of the gestures she and Martin would use. It included one in which the flat palm of her hand moved sharply to the front and then downward. "This one's important," emphasized Iris. "If you see this, stop what you are doing immediately!"

Will was astounded. "I can't believe I'm meeting two German folks who are fluent in Indian sign-language!"

"We also know the Lakota spoken language," said Iris with not a small amount of pride.

"So," said Iris, "when you find the exact location to bury your items, Martin and I will stand apart from you, but we will be sure to be where you can see us and where we can see a great distance as well. If we remain perfectly still, you continue to bury the items. Make sure you look up every so often! Remember, if either of us gives you the 'abandon' *Zeichen*… signal…then *halt!* You should stop what you are doing."

"This should not take long," promised Will. "I appreciate your help!" *Dankeschon!*"

When they arrived at Little Big Horn, Will and his new friends walked casually, taking time to read markers and memorials place by the Park Service. They finally came upon a location that Will thought would make a proper burial place for Hawk's artifacts. Iris and Martin each assumed their lookout positions, about fifty yards away. They looked in all directions for about half a minute and seeing no one, gave the "all-clear" signal.

Will unsheathed his knife, and used it to dig a depression about six inches deep. He placed the plastic bag in the shallow hole and covered it with dirt. He also took time to throw a few stones and twigs on top so that it wouldn't attract attention. Quickly, he rejoined Martin and Iris, and they continued their solemn walk through the battle site.

Two hours later the visit came to an end, and the German couple drove Will to the north bound entrance ramp of I-90. "Are you certain that someone will pick you up?" a concerned Iris asked.

"I've come this far with no problems," Will assured her. He had already prepared a sign that read, "Billings…please!" Martin and Iris agreed that the sign was an excellent idea.

"We will be going back to our hotel in Sheridan now," said Martin, "but first, we must take time for photos and exchange our addresses."

They assured one another that they would stay in touch. Already past noon, it was becoming uncomfortably warm. Will found a scrawny evergreen that would provide a modest amount of shade.

Before getting back into their car, Martin and Iris called out in unison a Lakota farewell: *"Tanjan Omani po!"* Of course the farewell was accompanied by a gesture!

CHAPTER 15

SOMEWHERE ALONG THE ROCKY MOUNTAIN FRONT, MONTANA

—⌒⌒—

80 million years ago during the Late Cretaceous, there began a period of mountain building in western North America known as the *Laramie progeny*. A major tectonic plate off the west coast began sliding eastward under the North America plate, causing a dramatic uplift of the thick mass above. Some 30 to 50 million years later, the process would culminate in the formation of a three thousand mile long "backbone" of North America. Repeated glacial erosion over the years would add a finishing touch to the project. Native Americans called the range *as-sin-wati* ("When seen from across the prairies, they looked like a rocky mass"). During the middle of the 18th Century, Europeans named them the Rocky Mountains.

Where the eastern slope of the Rockies collides with America's Great Plains is known as the Rocky Mountain Front. In his journal, Meriwether Lewis (Lewis and Clark expedition) tells us that the joy he experienced upon seeing the snowcapped Rockies for the first time was counterbalanced by his reflections on "the sufferings and hardships" the mountains would present to the Corps of Discovery on their way to the Pacific.

Nestled up against the Rocky Mountain Front some one hundred and fifty miles northeast of Missoula, stood a handsome log cabin of recent construction. Its pitched roof was capped with sturdy green metal more than capable of keeping Montana's whopping snowfalls at bay. Taking advantage of the surrounding beauty, a sturdy wooden deck wrapped three quarters of the way around the upper level. Some fifty feet behind the building stood an impressive wall of solar panels. The structure's 3,000 square feet of living space, impressive as it was, paled in comparison to many other Montana getaways being built by wealthy Californians and other out-of-staters. But if the well known maxim of the real estate industry, "location-location-location" was true, this was an exceptional property indeed.

For one thing, the structure could not be seen from the highway. The nearest paved road was over four miles away. There, a rustic appearing, but high-tech ranch gate guarded the entry road. A closer look would have revealed modern security features: surveillance cameras, intercom and a hydraulically operated heavy gauge steel gate. In addition to the usual cattle grating, an unseen tire spike mechanism lay buried at the entrance. Ominously, a metal sign read: **"Private Land. Trespassers Will be Shot"**. Those permitted entry would wind their way upward through magnificent stands of Engelmann Spruce and Lodgepole pines before arriving at the expansive meadow on which the house stood.

That evening, the lights were blazing. Parked in the driveway as well as randomly in the surrounding meadow, were twenty or so vehicles: pickups, four-wheel drive suburbans, some jeeps, several full-sized American sedans. All American vehicles, with one notable exception, a pristine black Mercedes-Benz Gelandeswagen.

One might assume a party was in progress, but there was no activity outside or on the decks, nor any music. The enormous Kalamazoo Outdoor Grill remained covered. Besides, what kind of party has armed men with walky-talkies stationed around the perimeter?

Guests were assembled in the great room… all men. At first glance, the room had the well-curated appearance of many homes of the wealthy. Impressive elk and moose trophies were prominently displayed, along with pronghorns and bighorn sheep. A magnificent Whitetail trophy hung on the center of the wall with a brass plaque announcing a Boone and Crockett score of 186. Giving the room a Museum Of Natural History look was a taxidermied mountain lion with bared teeth, artistically rendered atop an old bleached tree trunk and encased in glass. Expensive landscape paintings as well as high quality Navaho rugs and saddle blankets hung on the walls. A discerning eye couldn't miss the dynamic Remington bronze of a cowboy on a rearing horse. But only a true connoisseur would have recognized it as the one recently auctioned off at Sotheby's for $ 125,000.

But on some walls hung images not typically seen in mountain getaways. The sports memorabilia display included the iconic newspaper photo of a referee kneeling over a prone Joe Louis with a jubilant Max Schmeling in the background. Next to that was a more grainy, but equally notable image of big Jess Willard striding over the flattened Negro champ, Jack Johnson.

On another wall in Gothic print was the biblical verse: "The truth shall set you free". Beneath were photo portraits of notables such as Henry Ford with a quotation inscribed in the lower portion. A photo of Nobel Laureate James Watson with his quote, "all our social policies are based on the fact that their intelligence is the same as ours- whereas all the testing says not really". There was a signed photo of a smiling and handsome Randy Weaver with the admonishment, "Never forget Ruby Ridge!" Then came the even more sinister images of Hitler and Heinrich Himmler. Who was behind this eclectic—darkly eclectic—collection?

In the small library, comfortable and expensive leather chairs circled a glass topped table with an elk antler base. Very inviting, if you weren't repelled by the collection on the shelves. Yes, there were some mainstays for literary sportsmen such as Maclean's <u>A River Runs Through It</u> and an assortment of works by Hemingway, McGuane, Ruark and Kerasote. Surprisingly, a magnificent leather- bound, first edition copy of <u>Meditations on Hunting </u>by Jose Ortega y Gassett was included. If you stopped right here, the collection was quite impressive.

But again then came the darker side: well-worn copies of <u>Mein Kampf</u> stood out, along with with paperback editions of <u>The Protocols of the Elders of Zion</u> and multiple copies of Hernstein and Murray's <u>The Bell Curve.</u> A brand spanking new copy of <u>White Identity </u>by Jared Taylor appeared to have been added recently with a Post-it, "You gotta read this- Alan" affixed to the book's still pristine dust jacket. A couple hard-cover editions of <u>The Turner Diaries</u> written by William Luther Pierce under the pseudonym, "Andrew MacDonald" also sat on the shelves.

In the great room, three men sat at a table facing another dozen or so informally seated on a large couch and some folding chairs. A well-built man in his late forties presided. He stood behind a podium.

"Good evening, gentlemen. Your presence tonight speaks to your personal commitment to the cause. It warms my heart. If we didn't all share certain core beliefs, you wouldn't be here. We all recognize that the stand we take involves risk."

"But there's a difference between <u>holding</u> beliefs, and the willingness to <u>act</u> on them and make sacrifices in support of those beliefs. And as I've often reminded you, there's also a risk in NOT acting on your convictions … a risk to you…to your children…to the future of our beloved country. At some point history will judge us. We will either be looked upon as members of a generation that stood by and in the face of overwhelming evidence did NOTHING, or as those in the vanguard of a true patriotic movement that guided America back to its rightful destiny!"

There was a few seconds of silence before anyone spoke, a fellow named Del. His was a voice of skepticism. "It's not that I don't believe in what you're sayin', he agreed. "Hell, we all believe! It's just that we may be a little too late…"

"…too late, Del? Too late? Del, go back not so long ago, maybe when you were in school. Think about the TV programs you watched. Did you see black people reporting the news, or hosting shows? Black men hugging white women? Interracial couples flaunting their miscegenation ? Gay people behaving like sodomy is a perfectly normal thing? People on TV with names you can hardly pronounce from countries you never heard of?

Now take a close look at the people behind the entertainment and news media, the people promoting their perverted agenda… their twisted ideology. It's the liberal…mostly Jewish, I should add.. mostly Jewish writers and producers that are behind all the filth and so called multi-culturalism and …what are they always calling it…*diversity!* Rhymes with *perversity,* telling us that *mongrelization is* something to celebrate!"

"Just think about it. You look in the newspapers of Jew York and The Republic of *Kalifornicatia* and what do you read? Wedding announcements celebrating the coming union of Mary Jane and Betty Lou, between Neil and Bob. All this propaganda about the LGBTQWXYZ and who knows what else 'community'. Next thing you know they'll make bestiality legal... you know what that means, gentlemen? Do you? I don't think you do! It means cow-fucking!

"Many years ago—and you should know this stuff unless you slept through your history classes— the ancient Greeks developed a culture that was the envy of the world. They gave us architecture, philosophy, mathematical theories. Their achievements formed the foundation of what came to be known as Western Civilization. Do you know what caused the collapse of this wonderful civilization...and this is the part they never talk about in history class. Do you know what ended Greek Civilization?" The speaker paused, but there was no response. "OK then, I'll tell you what. It was when their men started butt-fucking boys. That's right. That you won't find it in your history books, and you can look all you want, because guess who writes those books? And besides, try teaching a high school class where that inconvenient piece of information has to be brought up!

The speaker then paused to look into the faces of the men around him. "I see some of you laughing. Well, laugh all you want, but I'm not making this up."

A growing murmur crept through the small assemblage. The man addressing them was clearly a gifted orator, some said he was a *natural,* the way he could first engage his listeners then enrage them.

"So I'm addressing what you say about being too late, Del. **It is not too late!** Not yet anyway. We still can save our country if we act now. But we must act. Soon. This change you are witnessing in our country, Del ... this change has all happened recently... within your lifetime actually. That's just the blink of an eye in the course of history. But it can be reversed just as quickly! Don't be telling me it's too late!"

The man again paused for a moment before raising his voice: "**Do any of the rest of you think it's ...*TOO LATE?*"** No one dared repeat the concern that it was "too late".

For a while, in fact, no one dared speak at all.

The men in the room were an eclectic group. Some were family men, but most were single. A few you could even call "loners" for whom the camaraderie provided a sense of belonging—to something, at least.

In terms of educational background, they ranged from high school dropouts to those with college degrees. Take Donny Jackson for example, one of the youngest of the group, sitting toward the back on a barstool. One of four brothers, he had dropped out of high school to work on the family ranch. His father, Vern Jackson III, was a fifth generation Montanan whose ancestors arrived in the territory two years before the Battle of Little Big Horn. By most accounts, Donny was not the brightest of the brothers. He had been attending these meetings for almost a year now.

Even an ex-felon sat in the room.

His name was Aaron Barber and his imposing mass occupied considerable space on the room's sprawling leather couch. Barber was a man in his mid thirties. His full beard and bulging muscles ostentatiously decorated with tattoos gave him the look of a gangster biker. Rumor had it that he had been involved in a methamphetamine operation in West Texas and had killed a member of a rival Mexican gang with his bare hands.

For that crime, Barber had spent eight years in the notorious Texas maximum security prison at Huntsville, the facility that houses the state's electric chair. While serving time, he became indoctrinated into White Supremacy ideology. Upon release from prison, an uncle up in Great Falls got him an interstate truck driving job. And a fresh start. Everyone deserves a second chance.

Within weeks after arriving in Montana, Barber was recruited by a group of men who recognized him as a kindred spirit.

They called themselves "The Front". The organization began about twenty five years ago. But since no one bothered to keep minutes during those early years, and since members disagreed over the semantics of what constitutes "a beginning", the precise date of their start was debatable. So members decided to simply embrace the shroud of mystery cloaking their origins. They all lived and worked on the eastern slope of the Rockies bordering the high plains, the Rocky Mountain Front. This name also held significance to a shared belief that they were in the vanguard of a movement. They called for a re-evaluation of the direction in which the nation was going, a re-awakening. With its metaphorical meaning, that chosen name, "The Front", held a certain appeal for the followers.

The man behind the podium, the charismatic self-appointed commander of The Front, was Tillman Lee Smith. He was a prominent local rancher and direct descendant of homesteader Hiram Smith who emigrated to the territory from Alabama in the late 1870s.

Generations of Smiths somehow managed to survive the rigors of Montana frontier life. Through the decades, natural disasters would periodically be visited upon them. They lived through cyclical droughts and those cruel winters like the ones in the late 1880s which took thousands of cattle. Many of the clan fled Montana during the severe economic downturn following The Great War. For those that stayed on, that legacy of continual hardship seemed to only strengthen their resolve...and maybe their orneriness.

Tillman Smith was not to be spared adversity either. In the early 1980s, his older brother Virgil was killed when his pickup was hit head-on by a car that swerved into the oncoming lane. The driver of that other vehicle, an undocumented Mexican, registered a .20 BAC at the time of the crash. He and his two passengers, also Mexicans, survived with minor injuries.

The tragedy had a profound effect on the family. Tillman's only other brother left Montana shortly after the accident. He was soon followed by the parents. In their nineties, they now live in an assisted living facility in Santa Rosa, California. Only a year after losing his brother, Tillman's marriage fell apart as well, leaving him to operate the ranch by himself with the help of hired hands.

Tillman and Virgil were only a year and a half apart in age and close in every other way. Some even say that Virgil was Tillman's best friend. Many will tell you how Tillman himself was never the same following that accident. That he had changed, always angry, developing a reputation as a loudmouth and a bully. Others say that one thing had nothing to do with the other, that he had always been that way. Just made it worse.

To set the proper course, The Front formulated a mission statement : To raise the consciousness and pride of all White brethren regarding the inherent role that race plays in our achievements. To support ongoing honest inquiry into the dangers of the false doctrines of <u>multiculturalism</u> and <u>diversity</u>. To ensure the biological and cultural survival of peoples of Northern European heritage and to protect the civil rights of the race that made America great.

But The Front was really two organizations, and this mission statement guided the activities of the organization's *inner sanctum,* it's white supremacy core. The other organization, the "public face" of The Front, was really a façade. It was that facade that most folks were familiar with, and it wasn't terribly different from other groups devoted to the promotion of patriotism, like the American Legion and numerous veterans associations. What could be wrong with that?

This dual identity of The Front was the brainchild of Tillman Smith. It would allow the more radical core to operate in secrecy, shielded by an idealistic and civic- minded public image.

"Let the public have that wholesome image," he instructed his *inner sanctum,* the *True Believers.* "It is unfortunate," Smith lamented, "that our most important work, the difficult task of saving America, has to take place behind closed doors."

"The day will come," he assured them, "in a more enlightened future, when we will be hailed as American heroes!"

How did The Front manage to keep its true mission hidden from the public? How did they maintain a wholesome patriotic image (what Smith facetiously referred to as *our Norman Rockwell persona)?* For one thing, the organization became a well-known sponsor of school and community projects. Recently, for example, an empty trash-strewn downtown lot had been transformed into a tastefully landscaped public park with seating areas and small tables. "Smith Community Park," read the bronze plaque fastened into a large boulder, "Thanks to the generosity of 'The Front' and the hard work of local volunteers"

Another such public relations initiative was The Front's annual essay contest for high school seniors. Over the years, announcement of the winner had become a much anticipated part of the end of the year awards assembly. Twenty five students of the most recent graduation class had submitted their thoughts, in five hundred words or less, on the subject, "Who is a True American?" A new Browning A-Bolt Stainless Stalker retailing for over $800, would be awarded to the winning writer.

The three person jury evaluating the submissions was made up of a high school dropout, a GED recipient and a junior college misfit who himself scored a paltry 202 on the verbal portion of the SAT. In front of a capacity crowd in the high school gym, the winning essay was described as "a masterpiece of plain talk and no big words." Tillman Smith himself was on stage to hand the beautiful weapon to the young author.

There was also the fact that membership into Smith's *inner sanctum* was by invitation only. An invitation from their commander. Once allowed entry, an oath of secrecy would be demanded Failure to abide by the secrecy oath carried harsh penalties. Penalties so gruesome, they remained largely unspoken. For years, an unconfirmed rumor circulated among them that several former members who had failed to live up to their oath were never seen again, though nobody seems to recall exactly who the vanished were. Nor did anyone dare suggest that the rumor may have originated with Tillman Smith. So far, the *real* organization had managed to operate behind the scenes, in the shadows.

Much of The Front's energy was devoted to fund raising. It seemed as if the organization never had enough money. Members were constantly being challenged to come up with creative schemes to raise capital: funds for the printing and distribution of pamphlets and "educational" literature, and most recently, money to launch a website/ discussion forum. A site to encourage open dialogue on issues related to right wing ideology. There was always that *mission statement.*

Like every organization, there were differences of opinion among the membership. For starters, not everyone in The Front was in favor that dual-identity strategy. Some saw no need in maintaining that all-American *Norman Rockwell* subterfuge. To tell the truth, this faction, the *hard-liners,* was losing patience with that cowardly charade. Most of the *inner sanctum* were present at that meeting a while back when one of the hard-liners stood up and boldly introduced the audacious idea of a kidnapping for ransom.

The suggestion came from a fellow whose attendance record at meetings was kind of on again-off again. Although known as Pete Anderson, at least one member seemed to recognize him from up in Cour d'Alene, Idaho, where he went by 'Pete Andrews' (as to the reason for an alias, one can only speculate, but all that speculation leads in only one direction).

Anyway, during that meeting, Pete defended the notion of kidnapping by proclaiming that "terrorism in the service of patriotism is 'righteous activism'"! The kidnapping idea itself was greeted with a mixture of laughter and whistling but also a scattering of "amens". But those words, *righteous activism*, did seem to have a profound ring to them.

Anderson had made the kidnapping suggestion under the influence of a fifth of Jack Daniels. But few knew that he had been pretty much shit-faced, since apparently no one had really ever seen him sober.

"I'm not talkin' about killing the guy," Anderson clarified, "although folks would have to be convinced that he really will die if the ransom money isn't received by a certain deadline. Of course, you would also have to make sure that the person comes from New York or California. That's where the money's at!"

Most members ridiculed the suggestion. But Anderson reminded them that their leader, Tillman Smith, had recently told everyone that risks would have to be taken, and that there was also a risk in NOT acting on your convictions. "You guys are pussy-footin' around with fucking essay contests," he yelled. "I'm talking reality!"

Tillman Smith, while taken aback by the outrageous suggestion, also realized that it takes many different kinds of people to make a movement like The Front successful. He didn't wish to alienate someone who might possibly serve a useful role in the future. Smith placated Anderson saying, "Well at least we got somebody here who's thinking outside the box! Let's hold off on Pete's suggestion until our next meeting. It's getting late."

So that meeting ended like they all did. Smith rose to his full height, once again taking his position at the podium. He gripped the edges, bent his head back slightly and looked upward to the vaulted ceiling. In what appeared to be a familiar and well-rehearsed practice, the men left their seats and stood before their commander with arms extended, palms down, in what appeared to be a fascist salute (the more astute might have also recognized it as the so-called Bellamy Salute used by thousands of American school children in the early twentieth century while reciting the "Pledge of Allegiance").

After a prolonged silence, Smith's lips began to quiver. His grip on the podium tightened. The recital began sonorously: *"Kein Hoschen halte mich, sha na na na na gekronte zeigen in verruckte Kartoffeln holen ergibt Bauschnitt schleppen bei Mir bist du shane. Lass uns zusammen kommen und fiel aulreit wie bissig fahren auf der Autobahn ein Reizhusten sehr stressig, sha na na na na, krum und grad, Wagenrad!"*

The monotone benediction went on and on before ending in a spent eyes-rolled-to-the- back-of-the-head orgasmic gasp.

And though the words never came out exactly the same, to his followers, the ritual was a familiar one. They truly believed their leader had been given the extraordinary ability to channel the ancient Nordic deities, the gift of pagan glossolalia. The dramatic performance would vary each time, sometimes lasting as long as five minutes, but the impassioned incantation of sumptuous guttural- sounding-utterances never failed to leave his followers…well, speechless!

But that night, at least one person allowed his mind to wander during Smith's benediction. Donny Jackson was still fixated on that notion of a kidnap for ransom. He didn't see it as a ridiculous suggestion. Not at all. And ever since joining The Front, a growing lack of respect from other members had been gnawing at him. That night, he saw an opportunity to elevate his status.

CHAPTER 16

LEAVING MISSOULA

---ᕦᕤ---

Time was you could get an inexpensive hotel room in Missoula, but that was then and this was now.

From under thirty thousand in the 1970s, the population had more than doubled by the early years of the new millennium. As the city grew, it gentrified. Many of the old downtown hotels, formerly places where drifters and folks down on their luck could get inexpensive lodging, were now chichi, with room rates to match. Will checked into a such a hotel and resigned himself to spending a bit more than planned by rationalizing that the splurge would be celebratory: he was finally in Montana, after all, "The Last Best Place"!

He had arrived in town early enough to take care of some shopping and pay a visit to the Museum of Arts and the Monty Dolack Gallery. Some time was spent in a favorite book store and he left with a Thomas McGuane paperback. Strolling the streets made Will curiously euphoric. Then again, the city had always done that to him, as did the State of Montana itself. He loved the state, and sometimes got the feeling that an entire life spent on Long Island, New York had been a geographical mismatch. With apologies to Billy Joel, Will soon found himself in a *Montana State Of Mind*.

That evening he made his way to the Top Hat, a favorite restaurant bar that he had enjoyed on previous visits. It lived up to expectations. A local band, "The Hippie Wranglers", was on stage, and the place was jumping. Determined to get a good night's sleep before his wilderness adventure, he left after the first set.

Next morning he left his small suitcase in safe-keeping with the desk clerk who's sign read *concierge*. Such language was obviously a way of justifying the exorbitant room rate. Will was on to that ploy of using fancy French or Italian vocab. In his neighborhood back in New York, as soon as Vincent's Italian Restaurant became *Ristorante Vincenzo,* the prices doubled.

He grudgingly handed a five dollar bill to Wyatt, the young man with a the *concierge* badge on the lapel of his ill-fitting suit jacket. "Please take good care of it, Wyatt. I should be back in town in a week to ten days to pick it up."

"Thank you Mr. Kraft. I hope you enjoyed your stay, and we look forward to having you as a guest once again." Wyatt scrutinized Will with a somewhat quizzical look. Not too many folks checked out of this hotel with a knapsack and hiking stick. *Maybe he was a German Tourist?*

With a sign that read, "Bob Marshall Wilderness…please!", Will walked out the door and headed to The I-90 East entrance ramp, where he hoped to get a ride to the Rte 200 North exit. In a mere ten minutes, a young couple from Wisconsin pulled over. They were on their way to Glacier National Park but would be going as far as Clearwater Junction today to visit relatives…would that work for him? Perfect said Will.

From that intersection he would have the option of heading straight north to a familiar trailhead at Holland Lake, or could continue west on Rte 200 and enter The Bob from the south or continue further still, and enter from a trailhead near Choteau, a small ranching community along the Rocky Mountain Front. Will liked the idea of having different options.

He was dropped off at the intersection of Rte 200 and 83 where a huge, kitschy fiberglass bull invited travelers into a favorite local café. Hungry, he accepted the invitation.

During breakfast he became involved in a conversation with a young fellow named Liam who offered to drive him in the direction of Choteau. Liam told Will that he couldn't take him all the way into Choteau, but would drop him off at an intersection about twenty miles from town.

Soon, they were on the road. Within a half hour, they entered the town of Lincoln where Liam slowed down to point out a sign, Twin Gulch Drive. "You know who used to live up that road?"

Of course Will knew. Liam was referring to probably the most famous… more to the point, infamous inhabitant of the small town. "You're probably talking about Ted Kaczynski, the 'Unabomber'."

"You knew that...how'd you know about that? I was only a little kid when all that happened, but I recall all the excitement. They say he was a real genius, but a sicko. If you want, I can take you up the road and show you where he lived."

Will didn't hesitate. "Maybe some other time. Right now I'm anxious to get into the mountains."

"No big deal," said Liam. "There's not much to see anyway. A while ago they hauled the cabin away and brought it to a museum in Washington DC."

"People are fascinated by that stuff, I guess," speculated Will.

"You know I was born and raised near here," explained Liam, "so were my parents. My grandparents immigrated from Norway back in the early 1900s, so we go back a ways. Don't get me wrong," he explained. "I love Montana and most folks are really good people, but the state does have its share of Wackos, people on the fringe."

"Every state has them," countered Will. "You think it's different anywhere else? Besides, you can't really call Kaczynski a Montanan. I think he was already in his thirties when he moved to your state."

"Then maybe the state attracts these people, or it could be because I live here, it just seems that way."

"Maybe. But you know what Liam? Everywhere you go, most folks are good people."

"I suppose," Liam agreed.

The conversation moved to other things like Liam's college career at the University of Montana, and the fact that he had made a decision to stay put and not move to the West Coast like a lot of his classmates. As always, time flew during conversation. Before you know, they came to the intersection where US 89 heads north.

Before farewells, Liam advised Will to stay at a place called "The Trail's End" in Choteau. "Mary Ann owns the place. She's my Aunt. Tell her that Liam Johnson sent you, and you may get a deal. No guarantee though, depends upon the kind of mood she's in."

They wished one another well, and Liam continued on to Great Falls. By then, it was already late morning and getting a little warm. Will walked over to a massive Cottonwood tree for some shade. You could never tell how long you would be standing alongside the road. He recalled times when he had to abandon the thumb in favor of the palms-together-in-prayer position. A friend once advised him if things get really desperate, try the kneeling-prayer position, something Will never had to resort to.

He would begin with the universally recognized thumb…and of course, a sign, "Choteau…please!"

Cars were far and few between. Conventional wisdom said that lone males were most apt to pick up a hitchhiker, but several had already passed by without so much as slowing down. It would make an interesting study, he thought: was there any correlation between getting picked up and the type of car you drove? Every so often he thought he had come upon some sort of theory only to see it dashed.

Maybe better that way, he thought to himself. If there were no real rules, then there would be no exception to the rules. So every approaching vehicle would be seen as a potential ride, and he would look in their direction, confidently!

CHAPTER 17

THE HUTTERITES

—⌇—

Innsbruck, Tyrol, The Holy Roman Empire. February 25, 1536.

Despite the pre-dawn chill, the public square was beginning to show signs of life. Awakening from their slumber, birds were busy collecting straw for their nests tucked into the eaves and crevasses of the city's structures. Merchants were setting up tables. Shopkeepers were sweeping their entranceways.

The first slanted rays of sun lit up the east face of the defensive wall that ringed the city. Over thirty years prior, a heraldic tower had been constructed in honor of the wedding of Emperor Maximillian I and Maria Sforza, daughter of the Duke of Milan. By the minute, the now famous golden roof tiles grew in brilliance.

Archduke Ferdinand I and his wife, Anna of Bohemia (and Hungary) would soon be seated in the famous loggia known affectionately as "der Goldenes Dachl" (the Golden Roof), to observe the event taking place today in the square. Though born in Spain, Ferdinand had been quick to learn that Austrians loved a spectacle. The square was frequently the scene of jousting matches, dancing and other performances. But on this day, something very special was to be staged for the good burghers of Innsbruck.

In the Hofburg, Ferdinand and Anna had already been awake for some time being tended to by the chamberlain and ladies-in-waiting. Ferdinand had not slept well, though he should have. After all, he was still basking in the glory of successive victories over invading Turkish armies led by Suleiman the Magnificent. At least for now, the Ottoman threat had been thwarted. Christianity had prevailed.

But a troubling new threat was now brewing from within the dynasty. All over Europe, radical thinkers such as Martin Luther, John Calvin and Huldrych Zwingli had begun to question the authority of the Roman Catholic Church, pointing out its corruption and hypocrisy.

The Anabaptist contingent (literally translated to"one who baptizes again") was one of the protesting groups. A fundamental tenet of their belief system was that the rite of baptism should be reserved only for those capable of freely choosing their confession of faith. Accordingly, they opposed infant baptism. Even more intolerable to the powers that be was their rejection of military actions. True believers, they said, would never bear arms or wield the sword. Even against wrongdoers.

Jakob Hutter of South Tyrol was among the many converts. A hat-maker by trade (Hutter means "hat-maker" in German), he became an Anabaptist as a young man and an ardent proselytizer of the belief system. His followers soon had an identity of their own. They became known as the "Hutterites".

Archduke Ferdinand of Austria was becoming increasingly concerned about the growing heresy. He made it clear that Hutterites and other reformers would not be tolerated. Hundreds were beheaded, drowned (mockingly referred to as the "third baptism") and burned at the stake. Many of Hutter's followers fled east to Moravia, where they sought the promise of religious tolerance.

For a while Hutterites did enjoy a respite from persecution, however, it did not last long. In many parts of Europe, they were forced into a nomadic existence.

Jakob Hutter became a wanted man. A reward of forty guilders, an average year's wage, was offered by Archduke Ferdinand for his capture. Finally, on November 29th, 1535, he, along with his wife Kathrina, were apprehended while on a missionary trip in Tyrol. He was taken to Innsbruck for trial.

Ferdinand at first was convinced he could persuade Hutter to see the error of his ways. He was interrogated, cajoled and whipped. Finally, he was placed on the infamous torture rack. Hutter continued to preach the gospel as his ligaments were stretched and his joints gave way, the loud popping sounds proclaiming a job well done to his tormentors.

Finally Ferdinand had had enough. *"Genug! Kein mehr Herr Nette Kerl, Jakob. Ich habe kein mehr Geduld!"* (Enough! No more Mr. Nice Guy, Jakob! I have run out of patience!) Apparently he had made up his mind anyway. He was heard to hiss to his confidants, "Even if Hutter should renounce the error of his ways, he will NOT be pardoned, for he has misled too many!"

Greater punishment awaited. Hutter was placed in freezing water, in abundant supply in the Alps during winter, then pushed into a hot room.

"Not a word of complaint, Jakob!" Ferdinand muttered. Then much to the great satisfaction of the sadists around him, the archduke added comic relief. "I'm told that in the Northern Lands, folks do this sort of thing regularly…for *Gesundheit (good health)!* Maybe for them, the hot room comes first, then the cold. How do they call it? *Sauna?"* The room erupted into laughter. No one dared *not* laugh.

Hutter's lips curved into a beatific smile as he contemplated joining his savior.

Though future historians would declare that the Medieval period had already evolved into the Renaissance, the carefully crafted torture methods (wasn't the Medieval period the golden age of torture?) were hardly forgotten.

Ferdinand's henchmen picked up their rods and began to beat Hutter, enough to inflict open wounds and keep him in agony. Then brandy was poured into the wounds… the cheap stuff, of course. He was immediately dragged out into the public square and tied to a stake. A pile of kindling and firewood was arranged neatly around him. The appointed time had arrived.

In the magnificent loggia, Ferdinand assumed a seat in his plush upholstered armchair. His wife, Anna of Bohemia (… and Hungary) then joined him. She had just given birth to her ninth child, Margaret, a few weeks before. Despite her weakened state, she was curiously attracted to spectacles of this sort. Of course, she was duty-bound as well.

How different was the burning of each heretic. Anna found it fascinating how some screamed in agony, while others endured their punishment stoically. At times, Anna pondered how she herself would fair if she were to be found guilty of witchcraft or adultery. What about this Hutter fellow? Would he provide the rabble with satisfying shrieks of agony, or would he remain disappointingly silent in the consuming flames?

These thoughts preoccupied her as she sat quietly at her husband's side.

The kindling was lit. Soon flames were licking at Hutter's still damp garments causing them to smolder for a time before igniting. At first the stench of burning flesh was apparent only to those closest to the pyre, but before long the familiar aroma would pervade the entire square. For a short while, Hutter's lips could be seen moving, still intently proselytizing, until his body finally shuddered and his eyes rolled to the back of his head. The final act did not go unnoticed by Anna.

She leaned forward and whispered into Ferdinand's ear, "I sometimes see your eyes roll back into your head when you achieve ecstasy. You don't suppose …?"

"You are a naughty vixen, Anna," Ferdinand played along. "Later this evening you will receive the spanking you deserve! For now, my dear, please conduct yourself properly!"

Over the course of the next three hundred years, Hutter's followers wandered throughout Europe, forming communal *Bruderhofs* (brotherhoods) from Tyrol to Moravia, to Slovakia and Transylvania, to Carinthia and Wallachia and finally the Ukraine. Alternately, they experienced periods of prosperity then economic ruin, decline and ascent. At times they were enthusiastically welcomed into new lands, at other times they were just tolerated at best and persecuted, at worst. Periods of war, which was much of the time, were especially difficult. Host countries could simply not accept the pacifism of the Hutterites.

In the late eighteenth and early nineteenth centuries, Hutterites finally found what they thought was their promised land (the earthly version), in Ukraine and Russia. Their communities grew in number as did their membership. They became the envy of locals for their prosperous industries and agricultural prowess. Internal strife however, threatened their fundamental belief system. Indeed their very survival was threatened. A persistent disagreement festered over whether to maintain a "community of goods" lifestyle, or allow individual ownership.

In the middle of the nineteenth century, with leadership from Johannes Cornies and then Michael Waldner and Jakob Hoffer, the community of goods concept was re-established and Hutterites as a group were re-invigorated. Then once again, their belief in pacifism caused them trouble. Russia had made new regulations requiring compulsory military service for everyone. No exceptions.

In response, Hutterites Paul and Lorenz Tschetter, set out to North America in search of yet another promised land.

Alarmed at the possible departure of forty five thousand industrious farmers, the Russian government sent a delegation to persuade them to stay. Despite entreaties, the Hutterites decided to emigrate. And so, this tribe of adult-baptizing pacifists arrived on our shores, exchanging the steppes of Ukraine for the prairies of North America...the Eastern Hemisphere for the Western.

Then came the Great War. Once again the Hutterite commitment to pacifism created problems for them. That old bugaboo that plagued them for centuries in Europe now reared its ugly head in the US of A!

Speaking German at a time of rabid anti-German hysteria, a cloud of suspicion soon hung over Hutterite communities. Pacifists through and through, they not only refused to wear military uniforms, but also refused to contribute any money to help finance the war. If young Hutterite men were conscripted, they would refuse to perform military duties or don a uniform. As a result, some were beaten and tortured in training camps.

One infamous case involved Jacob Wipf and the three Hofer brothers, Joseph, Michael and David. Because of perceived insubordination, they were sent to Alcatraz where mistreatment escalated, resulting in the deaths of Joseph and Michael. The brothers now lay buried in South Dakota in their Rockport Colony Cemetery with the word "Martyr" inscribed on their grave markers.

Persecution during WWI and afterward led most Hutterites to flee for the relative safety of Canada. It was only after World War II and the cooling off of anti-German sentiment that many began returning to Montana. Among the first wave of returnees was the Miller family with their eight children, five girls and three boys. Hal was the youngest. Now in his sixties, he had risen to a position of leadership in his colony, a "Boss."

Hal had just spent the morning at a business meeting in Great Falls. He was driving his pickup back to the colony near Choteau. The meeting went well, and his spirits were high.

CHAPTER 18

A HARMONIC CONVERGENCE

A person's history accompanies him in all circumstances. Whenever strangers'paths cross— a so-called "chance meeting"—a confluence of cultures and backgrounds takes place like two separate circles converging in a Venn diagram. In much the same way that the collision between the Missouri River and the mighty Mississippi results in a river forever changed, so can human lives be forever changed.

On this Friday in late June, Hal Miller was behind the wheel of his old Ford pickup heading back to the colony after finishing up some business in Great Falls. A conservative man, he maintained a conservative speed. Secretly, however, he often fantasized about racing a car down Montana's empty highways at daring speeds. Just like he had seen in Hollywood movies. He even fantasized about participating in a Cannonball Run Race across the United States. Of course, he never acted on such fantasies, nor did he dare share them with anybody...he was after all, a Hutterite.

It was already late morning when he approached the fork in the road where US 89 veers off from Rte 200 and heads in the direction of Choteau. Ahead of him, in the shadow of an old Cottonwood, stood a youngish man with a hiking stick, a backpack and a sign that read, "Choteau...please!"

Maybe it was the hiking stick that gave the fellow a biblical visage, like a shepherd with his staff. Or maybe it was Hebrews 13:2, "Be not

Erwin. (Erv) Krause

forgetful to entertain strangers; for thereby some have entertained angels unawares." One of of Hal's most beloved passages from the Old Testament, it immediately came to mind when he saw the hitchhiker. So many of his decisions had been informed by scripture.

He flicked on the turn signal and pulled over. Through the open passenger window he asked, "Where you going to?"

"To Choteau," Will replied. "Hopefully to get a room at the Trail's End."

"Trail's End? That's Mary Ann's place. Do you know her?"

"No, but I did meet her nephew, Liam. He recommended I spend the night there."

"Well if you never met her, you're in for a treat," laughed Will. "Hop In then. I'm heading back to the colony, but I can drop you off in town. It's hardly out of my way." He spoke with that faint German accent that Hutterites had.

Will placed his backpack and hiking stick in the bed of the pickup and jumped in, taking a quick glance at the driver. His full beard, and black hat and suspenders were classic Hutterite. Will had seen these folks on previous travels, and he once stopped at a colony to buy vegetables.

Will reached over to shake hands, "Will Kraft. Thanks for the lift!"

"Hal Miller," said the driver, grasping Will's hand firmly.

As soon as they drove off, they began to chat, small talk initially. Within a few minutes though, Will was asking many questions about the Hutterites and their history. Hal obliged him with enthusiasm.

"If I seem overly curious," Will said apologetically, "I should tell you that I'm a history teacher *or at least I used to be.* I'm especially interested in European History."

"History teacher are you?" That piece of information seemed to get Miller's attention. With a mischievous twinkle in his eyes, he looked in Will's direction. "OK then, I got a history question for you: who was the only person in congress to vote against a declaration of war in both World Wars, I and II?"

"That would be Jeanette Rankin," replied Will without hesitation, "congresswoman from Montana."

"Right you are, Will! Miller giggled. "Maybe we should have made her an honorary Hutterite. One of the pillars of Hutterite faith is pacifism… but you probably already knew that."

"That I knew," replied Will, "but there is an awful lot I don't know."

"In that case, let me ask you something. Are you in a real hurry to get to Choteau?"

"A hurry? Will pause briefly. "Not really…"

"Well then, how'd you like an all-expense-paid-tour of my colony? We'll be getting there just in time for lunch. Would you like to be my guest?"

"Hal, I would love that!"

"Alright! Then sit back and relax. And learn," Hal invited. "As a history teacher, you probably know something about the Protestant Reformation and the religious strife of the sixteenth and seventeenth centuries, but how much did you learn specifically about the Hutterites?"

"Not that much, I'm afraid…"

"Then let me tell you a few things about us 'Hoots'…"

From that point on, Hal talked nonstop. Will received a crash history course that began with the Anabaptist movement, its belief in the Community of Goods and the biblical basis for those beliefs. Hal also spoke of the persecution that Hutterites suffered at the hands of Roman Catholics and others, about their migrations across Europe and how they eventually wound up in North America. While Hal continued his tutorial, Will thought about all the college courses he had taken, and all the lectures he sat through. None had the authenticity of the one he was now getting in the front seat of an old pickup truck in Montana.

They arrived at the colony just before lunch. Hutterite settlements all shared pretty much the same design. Throughout the USA and Canada, each was a self-sufficient, independent economic unit. They had a reputation for being well-managed and efficient, producing a far greater share of agricultural product than most farms their size. In fact, the fifty or so Hutterite colonies in Montana produced almost 90% of the state's hogs and a whopping 95% of its eggs!

Each family had its own modest living quarters with a neatly trimmed patch of lawn and clothing drying rack in the front. No garden gnomes allowed! The largest building on the grounds was the communal dining hall, where food was prepared by the women. Labor was neatly divided by gender.

In the dining hall, Will sat next to Hal at a table of men. The stuffed cabbage was as good if not better than the Halupki that Annie's mother had prepared a while back. Of course, he would never share that fact with Laura... ever! *Was it possible that almost a week had passed since he sat with Annie in her parents' dining room in Austin?* Homemade dinner rolls were served with the stuffed cabbage. They had a slight sweetness and a lovely glaze.

Following lunch, Hal invited Will to see the school. Though classes were not in session, Will did get to meet one of the teachers, Mrs. Hofer, who was working on future lessons and activities. "Did Hal explain to you that the folks in this colony are part of the 'Lehrerleut' group," she asked, "which literally means 'Teacher-People'?"

Will exchanged information with Mrs. Hofer and promised to touch base with her when he got back to Long Island. She promised to reciprocate. He thought he might even incorporate a lesson about the Hutterites when they were covering the topic of religious freedom *If I ever step foot in a classroom again, that is.*

After Hal showed Will the rest of the compound, they got back into the pickup and drove into Choteau. They pulled up in front of the little motel owned by Liam Johnson's aunt. After thanking Hal and retrieving his gear from the pickup bed, Will stepped into the office.

Seeing no one, he rang the little dome shaped bell sitting on the counter. From behind a beaded curtain entranceway came a hoarse-voiced, "Be with you in a second." Two minutes later, a thin-as-a-rail woman redolent of tobacco smoke, stepped out. She could have been a real looker back in her day, but the creased face and whiskey voice suggested a history of dubious lifestyle choices.

"Looking for a place to stay?"

"Yes I am," Will responded. "Non-smoking, if you don't mind."

"We got rooms where everyone smokes and a few where only some smoke. Take your pick. You got a pet?"

"No pet."

"Too bad, 'cause there's no extra charge for them, so you probably would be better off with one, if you get my point."

"I get your point. By the way, your nephew Liam Johnson recommended your place…he told me to mention that."

"That might've helped last week, but Liam still hasn't paid back the twenty dollars I loaned him, so right now he's on my 'shit list'!"

Will quickly countered, "In that case I should tell you that I'm no friend of Liam's…does that get me a discount?"

"Nice try, hon! Thirty two dollars. Get Liam to pay up his debt, I can do better."

"I'll certainly remind him when I see him again," promised Will.

"OK then— refresh my memory—smoking or less smoking?"

After showering, Will found his favorite shirt buried in the bottom of his backpack. He put it on and strolled over to The Jackelope, a favorite local watering hole not far away. On his way, Will looked up at the many false front commercial buildings that lined the main drag. The architecture left little doubt that he was in the American West.

After opening the entrance door of the establishment, Will encountered one of those swinging saloon doors. He half expected someone to greet him with, "Howdy stranger. You're not from around these parts, are you?" That didn't happen. Maybe as a kid he had watched too many Westerns.

The interior featured prototypical western décor. Not-too-bad cowboy art included a few Charley Russell reproductions and of course, the obligatory horns and antlers from local ungulates. Will smiled as he read some of the hokey signs and their folksy words of wisdom: "If you're drinking to forget, please pay in advance" and "Patrons discussing sports, politics and fly fishing, do so at their own risk".

Will would always enter bars with the noble intention of leaving after a beer, or two at most. Too often, it didn't work out that way. Actually, his success rate in that department was less than stellar. Two beers had a way of leading to a third and then another… and well, you know how it goes. What is it they say about the road to hell being paved with good intentions? That would not happen tonight, he promised himself. Tomorrow morning he would get an early start, he promised himself. He would be in The Bob when the sun rose… he promised himself.

The young lady behind the bar greeted him with a smile. She was a raven-haired beauty with tight jeans and one of those fancy, snug-fitting floral pattern western shirts with a stylized yoke and shiny snap buttons. The top three buttons not fastened and probably never had been. She had a way of leaning forward, making guys feel special when she asked if they wanted another beer. How could they say no?

The rawboned cowboy sitting next to Will looked as if he had spent more time on a barstool than in a saddle. He leaned over to Will and shared, "Disgraceful isn't it, how young ladies today flaunt their 'cleavaredge'!"

"Funny, I didn't notice," affected Will. Then as an afterthought, "Whatever happened to modesty?"

They both enjoyed a laugh.

"To modesty," the cowboy raised his glass, "may it never again rear its ugly head! Name's Slim Bradshaw by the way," putting his glass down to shake Will's hand.

Before long, a tall, lanky fellow who Will hadn't noticed before, joined the conversation. Donny was his name, and within a few minutes he was buying Will a beer. Then a few more. Soon this Donny fellow managed to steer the conversation away from *cleavaredge* to the subject of second amendment rights. A couple of Olympias later (...or was he drinking Raniers?), Will decided to opine on the subject. *Patrons discussing politics do so at their own risk.*

What Will said went something like: Well, I'd like to respectfully disagree with the notion that any American should be able to go and buy an automatic or semi-automatic weapon with a large capacity clip which is something that really belongs only in the hands of military and as a nation we would be better off with some modest, sensible gun-control legislation which wouldn't take guns out of the hands of law-abiding citizens as long as they submit to background checks and take a gun safety course after all we all have to take a test to get a driver's license don't we and I still support the right to bear arms as stated in our constitution but I don't think the founding fathers had any way of knowing that things would lead to what we have today so let's use some common sense which I think most sportsmen would agree with.

Anyway, something like that.

Discussing gun control in a western bar is by definition, imprudent. Will should have known better. But ill-advised as it was, he recalled thinking that he had navigated those treacherous waters quite well. Didn't he say that he supported the right to bear arms? Had he disregarded Annie' suggestion that his comments should be more "filtered"? *Maybe he was a slow learner.*

As for Donny, who appeared to be listening attentively to what Will had to say, he really heard only one thing: "gun control – good!"

Later, Will would recall that four or five beers had never quite affected him quite the way they did that night. Maybe it was the altitude? But at only 3'000 feet above sea level? Maybe not.

CHAPTER 19

RIGHTEOUS ACTIVISM

———⌒⌒———

Funny how some days start out so well and then go rapidly downhill. Donny Jackson woke up in a great mood. He should have. It was Friday, the beginning of his weekend, and a glorious summer day to boot. It was at the breakfast table things began to change.

While finishing up his bacon and sunny side-up eggs, his father reminded Donny that he hadn't yet repaired the muffler on his car. "A month ago you said you would do it. Don't be promising to do something for me and then don't do it, Donny!"

"OK, Dad, OK! I'll do it!" Donny replied with resentment. Since his older brothers had gotten married and had families, it seemed that all the dirty work was left up to him.

Then he started thinking about his ex- girlfriend, Gretchen. They had been together for over a year, then a few weeks ago she dumped him for Pete Schoonmaker, a college graduate with a better job. How did she put it, that he was a "better prospect" or something like that. Not that she had the guts to tell him face to face. No, he had to hear it from one of his friends, which made it even worse. That betrayal was back on his mind.

Then his father brought up a growing bone of contention. "You know, Donny, if you would spend less time with Tillman Smith and that bunch, maybe you could make something of yourself. Not to mention get some things done around here!"

Whenever the subject of Tillman Smith came up, Donny reflexively come to the man's defense. "What Tillman and that 'bunch' are doing is important," Donny proclaimed, "even if you don't want to admit it!"

"Donny, maybe you need reminding that I grew up with Smith. He was a bully and a blow-hard in high school, and he's the same now! No, actually he's worse. I hear how he talks. And lately showing up in town with that big-ass Mercedes Jeep, acting like a big shot. The other day he took up two parking spots in the parking lot so his car don't get dinged. And a while back I saw him parked in a handicapped spot. I stopped and looked at him. He looked back at me as if to say, 'What are you going to do about it?' I just shook my head and walked on by."

"Dad, could it be you're just a tad jealous? Maybe 'cause he's running a successful ranch and can afford that car."

"Just fix the damn muffler like you said you would," Donny's father growled.

The muffler repair job turned out to be more involved than planned. Of course. These jobs always do. And Donny got a lot dirtier than planned. By the time he finished it was seven o'clock.

During supper, his dad asked what are you doin' tonight, Donny.

"Having a beer or two at the Jackelope."

"Don't get home too late. You know I'm going to need some help tomorrow fixin' that fence along the irrigation ditch."

"Tomorrow's Saturday, Dad," Donny whined.

"I don't need no remindin' what day it is, Son!"

And this is how things had been going lately between him and his old man. Donny stormed from the table. *Some day,* he brooded to himself, *people will find out that I was meant for more important things than mufflers and fence mending!*

Donny showered, splashed on some after- shave and got dressed. He left the house and slid behind the wheel of his pickup. It was past eight o'clock when he entered The Jackelope. Only one vacant barstool remained. It was Friday night after all. He took a bee-line to the bar and looked around. He pretty much recognized every face there.

But there was at least one unfamiliar face, a gentleman sitting at the bar laughing and shooting-the-shit with Slim Bradshaw. Bradshaw was an on again-off again wrangler who had a habit of disappearing for months at a time. I wonder when Slim got back in town, thought Donny. A confirmed bachelor, Bradshaw was known to have a serious crush on the barmaid, Marlene Nelson. Then again, so did every heterosexual male in the place.

Marlene leaned over to Donny. "What're you drinking tonight, Donny?" Of course she knew, since he had never requested anything other than an Olympia beer, but you never know. And of course, Donny already knew what he would ask for as well. But he would always, oh so cleverly, take time to cogitate a response, allowing him time to scrutinize the marvelous soft white swelling contending with the snap buttons on her stylish Western shirt. Patient as always, Marlene would await Donny's reply. *Don't think I don't know what you're up to, you horny bastard.*

"I guess I'll have an Oly tonight, Marlene."

"How'd I know that, Donny?" Marlene replied sarcastically as she turned to retrieve his beer. In less than thirty seconds, she returned with Donny's request, which was placed on his coaster in a bosomy encore. Tips were an important part of her income.

Half the glass was emptied in the first gulp. He had probably sweated off a few gallons today, replacing that damned muffler. That first beer always went down so easy. Sometime into his second Oly, Donny joined the conversation with the stranger and Slim Bradshaw.

"Where you from?" Asked Donny.

"New York...Will is my name."

"From *New Yawk*?" chuckled Donny. Although his attempt at mimicking Newyorkese was rather pathetic, Will got the point and politely joined Donny in laughter.

"New York the city, or New York the state? Folks say there's a big difference." Asked Donny.

"Just outside the city on Long Island," clarified Will.

"*Lawn Guyland?*" joked Donny again, pronouncing it the way he had heard them say it back there. In truth, no one had said it that way in over fifty years. How many times had Will heard that... "*Lawn Guyland?*" But he laughed anyhow, not wishing to slight the young fellow.

"Ever get mugged?" persisted Donny, continuing to play the stereotype card.

"You know, a lot of people ask me that," Will said thoughtfully, "but New York is a lot better these days. Tell you the truth though, even my dad, who lived in The City during the 'bad old days' back in the seventies and eighties...he never got mugged."

Slim then re-entered the conversation, which then jumped around from topic to topic before settling on gun control. Donny shared that the reason he had never been to New York was because he'd been told that it was actually against the law to bring a handgun into the city.

"Bringing a handgun would not be a good idea, Donny! Actually bringing any kind of gun into New York City would be a mistake," confirmed Will.

"Probably your *Jews* passed those laws!" Donny concluded emphatically.

"I'm not so sure what Jews had to do with it," protested Will, now wishing to steer the the discussion in another direction.

Donny remained persistent. "How many white folks actually are there in New York anyway, with all your Hispanics, your Blacks, your Orientals..." then paused and looked into Will's eyes, "...your Jews?"

At that point, Slim rolled his eyes, put down a generous tip for Marlene and got off his barstool. "I'll let you guys solve the problems of the world!" he laughed before disappearing out the door.

Will couldn't let Donny's remark go without rebuttal. "Donny, New York is certainly different, but trust me, if you ever come to the city, you'd realize that people are quite friendly. Hey, I gotta take a leak. Where's the men's room?"

Will was directed to the far end of the establishment where two doors stood side- by -side, "Bucks" and "Does".

When Will left to go to the bathroom, Donny saw an opportunity. He desperately wanted to elevate his status in Tillman Smith's Front organization and was still fixated on Pete Anderson's words at the last meeting. What did he say? Something about ...*righteous activism*...and the challenge to stop *pussy-footin' around*. Besides, this Jew-boy, Will... *funny, he don't look Jewish*...was starting to get on his nerves with his New York attitude.

Donny got the attention of lovely Marlene. "Another Oly for my friend here, please?" pointing to the empty barstool next to him.

Marlene poured the beer and set it down on the coaster. Donny reached into his pocket, took a quick look around and adroitly slipped a little green Rohypnol pill into Will's beer. Seconds later, Will was back on his stool. Donny then generously bought Will another, and still another.

Donny then resurrected the subject of gun control. Slurring his words, Will responded in the form of an overly-long, disjointed but passionate rant.

Now he's really starting to piss me off! Thought Donny.

In another twenty minutes, Will was slumped over the bar. Marlene observed sympathetically, "I don't think your friend needed that last beer or three!"

Donny feigned sympathy, "Don't worry, Marlene. He's stayin' at MaryAnn's place. I'll make sure he gets back safe!"

"You're such a sweetheart, Donny!" Marlene smiled.

*Did she just call me…sweetheart…*thought Donny.

The Jackelope was pretty much empty by the time Good Samaritan Donny Jackson provided Will with much needed assistance. He placed Will's arm around his shoulder and half dragged- half walked him out to the parking. There he gently placed him into the passenger side of the pickup, started the engine and slowly drove to the Trail's End.

At the motel, Donny carefully removed the room key from the pocket of his very unconscious passenger, quietly opened the door and let himself in. He gathered Will's possessions, threw everything into the bed of the pickup and drove off. He glanced over at Will who was breathing heavily and drooling out of the side of his mouth.

So pathetic, smiled Donny, *so very pathetic.*

CHAPTER 20

KIDNAPPED!

When Will finally came to, it was pitch black. Lying on a cold concrete floor, there was an execution-type blindfold hood over his head, and his hands were zip tied behind his back. A rag had been stuffed in his mouth, held in place with duct tape. He struggled to get his to get his feet underneath him and quickly realized that his wrists were hog-tied to his ankles. On a positive note, his violent headache informed him that he was at least still alive.

On his knees, he managed to shuffle across the floor until he came to what felt like a door. Pounding his head against the door oddly provided some relief from the headache. Between that and his muffled yells, he got someone's attention.

"Sounds like our Jew-boy's got something to say," came a mocking voice from the other side of the door.

"Don't they always," added another voice, followed by guffawing.

The door opened. Will was grabbed under his armpits and half dragged, half carried a few feet before being dropped on to a carpeted floor. Will soon realized that the more he struggled, the tighter the zip ties became.

Someone quipped, "Let's see how long it takes the genius to figure out that the more he fusses, the more entertainment we get!"

That voice, thought Will, *that young man's voice…why does it sound so familiar?* Then it came to him. Could it be that fellow "Donny", his drinking buddy at the Jackelope last night ?

He became outraged. Not just at those enjoying themselves at his expense, but more at his own stupidity for getting into this situation.

Then he detected approaching footsteps followed by a new voice, deeper and more authoritative. "Now be nice son, be nice! That's a Louisville Slugger you got there…go easy!"

Will attempted a defensive crouch, the futility of which evoked a burst of snickering. *You had to hand it to these guys…they knew how to have fun.* He sensed that someone was standing over him. Judging from the chant, "Home run! Home run!", he gathered that his tormentor had assumed a batting stance.

The deep voice quickly restored order. "Alright son, you had your fun. The party is over!"

This was followed by, "Everyone else! If I didn't ask you to stay, go home!" There came a somber warning, "You are reminded of the code of silence!"

There was a shuffling of feet, some parting laughter and disappointed murmuring as the lesser underlings departed. Then there was silence.

Will lay there for what seemed an eternity, but was actually only a half hour or so. He was dragged back to the concrete floor, and the door slammed behind him. "What was the point of all that," Will thought to himself. "Am I some sort of trophy? A nice eight point buck someone just bagged? *What the hell was going on here?*

How long he lay on the cold surface he could not say, but it probably felt much longer than it really was. He could make out snippets of conversation from the adjoining room. At one point, a loud voice insisted, "No, no, no… that's not how we do things!" Then came a more ominous, "We've come this far already… why not…"

They were clearly deciding his fate.

Will struggled to fight back a sense of panic. Thoughts of his children seemed to help. He had to get himself out of this mess for them.

Another half hour or so went by before he heard the squeaking of door hinges and the sound of footsteps. The deep voice again. "How did our guest behave?" Only then did Will realize that someone had been watching over him this whole time. Did they think he could possibly escape? *That he was Harry Houdini?*

Will was once again dragged back into what he heard them call the "Conference Room". He heard chairs being moved about, men getting seated. That much he could figure out. Then the leader announced, "OK, let us begin, Mr. Kraft. We have much to talk about." They knew who he was. Of course they did. They had his wallet.

Will managed a grunt through the duct tape.

"I suppose conversation will flow more smoothly if we remove that gag", suggested the man with the deep voice, the leader of The Front, Tillman Smith. "That would help, don't you think, Mr. Kraft? And when we remove it, Mr. Kraft, you won't yell or scream or anything foolish like that, will you? Shake your head 'no' for us to tell us that you won't do anything foolish. Can you please do that for us... MR. KRAFT?"

Will was infuriated by the exaggerated faux politeness and that overblown way of repeatedly addressing him by last name, with its mocking formality. This man was letting Will know just who was in charge.

Angered and terrified, what choice did he have except to obey. Again, he could sense approaching footsteps, then heard the click of a folding knife. He felt the tugging of tape against his cheeks and nape of his neck as the blade sawed through. The gag came free! But he experienced little relief.

"What about the hood?" Will muttered.

"Do you really want that, Mr. Kraft?" asked Smith, feigning surprise. "Do you really want to be able to recognize us? You surely understand how that would place you in a compromising position. Need I explain? For your own protection, Mr. Kraft..." He had a point.

"Look, what the hell is this all about?" Will pressed.

"We're getting to that, Mr. Kraft... please be patient."

"How many of you are there... can I at least know that?"

"I suppose it wouldn't hurt for you to know that there are five of us. You make six. Only one of the six is unarmed by the way. And who do you think that would be, Mr. Kraft? The man taunted.

"There's yet another difference between us, "he went on, "a political difference. You see, Mr. Kraft, my colleagues and I are ardent supporters of our Constitution, but it appears that you, on the other hand, have some reservations about the wisdom of our founding fathers and that sacred document."

Smith paused before asking, "You do believe in American Exceptionalism, don't you, Mr. Kraft?"

"Of course! I'm proud of my country!"

"Well you may say that, but at least one of my colleagues here thinks you are less than patriotic..."

"Damn right!" interjected that familiar voice. "Shit, not just unpatriotic, but probably a card-carrying 'communis'... like most Jews!"

"Now calm down, son," Smith intervened. "Let's try to help Mr. Kraft refresh his memory."

A smile crept across Smith's face Tillman Smith, a calculated smile. Years of bullying had taught him that more damage was inflicted by laughing at someone, than by hurling insults. He was the ultimate alpha male. Blindfolded as he was, Will could not *see* the smile...but he could *hear* it.

"Mr. Kraft, do you recall a conversation you were a part of last night at the Jackelope Saloon?" Smith questioned, "or perhaps you were too inebriated to recall the evening's festivities. Here, I'll give you a little hint: it had to do with the Second Amendment." After a short pause, Smith pushed further. "By the way, can you even tell us what the Second Amendment is?"

"Of course!" Will insisted. "It's the amendment giving Americans the right to bear arms..."

"No, no, no," Smith ridiculed, "any junior high student knows that! I mean can you actually recite the amendment word-for-word?"

"Word-for-word?" answered Will. "Maybe not exactly word-for-word, but..."

Smith abruptly interrupted, "Somehow I didn't think you could! So I will educate you. And I expect you to listen carefully…and respectfully, Mr. Kraft…respectfully!"

Smith paused, took a deep breath and pedagogically recited, "A WELL REGULATED MILITIA, BEING NECESSARY TO THE SECURITY OF A FREE STATE, THE RIGHT OF THE PEOPLE TO KEEP AND BEAR ARMS, SHALL NOT BE INFRINGED."

"Why din't you know that? I thought Jews were s'pposed to be smart!"

Now Will knew for sure. That voice *did* belong to Donny.

Another man with kind of a Jimmy-crack-corn timbre kept mumbling something about if *these people* had only accepted the Lord Jesus as their savior, they wouldn't be in this situation. It was the same line of reasoning used five hundred years earlier during the the Spanish Inquisition to squeeze the Jews. But this was the Twenty First Century…*Did people still think this way?*

"Look, I may not know the whole thing by heart, the Second Amendment…" Will objected. "But anyway, why do you guys keep calling me a Jew? What makes you think I'm Jewish?"

"What makes me *think* you're a Jew?" Donny retorted. "I don't *think*, I KNOW! You talk like a Jew, you look like a Jew…sort of…, you act like one, you got a Jewish last name! You want me to go on?"

"What the hell does a Jew sound like when he talks?" Will yelled.

"Don't ask me to imitate Jew-talk," protested Donny. "I can't do that, but they all got that smart-ass-Jew-York way of talking…I watch TV!"

"…like Seinfeld?" Will baited.

"Yeah, like Seinfeld now that you brought it up! Donny shouted.

"Look," Will yelled back, "I can't help I'm from New York and how I talk, and not that it would make any difference with you guys anyway… but I AM NOT JEWISH!"

A pause followed as the men looked at one another questioningly. Then they scrutinized Will. One suggested running a hand across Will's scalp. "There might be horns," he explained. No one took him up on that suggestion, but two men did step somewhat closer to Will, hoping to discover physiognomic subtleties that might offer some clues. "You can't really tell with that blindfold covering his nose," complained one.

Tillman Smith took charge once more. He stepped up to Will. Enunciating each word with care, he asked, "Are you Christian, Mr. Kraft?"

"Don't let him talk his way out," cautioned Donny

"Shut up, son!" snapped Smith, his annoyance with Donny now clearly showing. Then once again, he turned to Will. "I ask once more, Mr. Kraft, ARE. YOU. CHRISTIAN?"

Will had given up Christianity and pretty much all organized religion during his college years and now thought of himself as agnostic. Still, he didn't relish the notion of martyrdom in the cause of agnosticism. He also wisely decided that this was not a good time to enter a theological debate. Clutching at the straw presented to him, he boldly proclaimed, "I was baptized Lutheran. I AM CHRISTIAN!"

Maybe it was a remnant of Christianity remaining in him. But at the moment he uttered those words, he was convinced that he would be struck by lightning for the shamelessness of his falsehood.

Then the men started arguing amongst themselves. Above the tumult, Will heard Donny's protests. "Right there you got your proof that he's a Jew f'sure… and a lyin' Jew at that!"

"Shuddup, son!" Smith demanded. "I'll be doing the inquisiting here!" Decorum slowly returned.

Then came something totally unexpected. Tillman Smith suddenly issued a command to his men: "PULL DOWN HIS PANTS!"

"Whaaat!...?"

"You heard me," Smith confirmed. "I said pull down Mr. Kraft's trousers! Cut those zip ties so he can stand up, THEN PULL.DOWN. HIS.PANTS!"

The demand was issued uncharacteristically loud for Smith. Was he losing control of the situation? Someone dared question the decree. "Boss, I know where you're going here, but just cause he's 'circumscribed' don't prove he's a Jew or not!"

"CircumCISED! circumCISED!" Smith corrected. "But on the other hand, if he's not... and the word is 'circumCISED'...it would prove beyond doubt that he is NOT Jewish, wouldn't it?"

Smith paused and stepped toward Will. Will could feel the man's warm breath against the side of his face as he argued, "One would think that Mr. Kraft here would welcome the opportunity to show us convincingly that he is not a Jew." Smith then paused for a moment, glared at Will, then raised his voice again, "ISN'T. THAT. RIGHT...MR. KRAFT?"

At this point, Will completely lost it. He shouted, screamed actually, "You know what I think? You really want to know? I think you're all SICK PUPPIES, that's what! You. All yourselves patriotic Americans, and you're pulling shit like they did in NAZI-FUCKING-GERMANY!"

He had plenty more to say, but a hard open hand to the face put an end to his rebuttal.

"Do as I ordered," snarled Smith. "PULL. DOWN. HIS. PANTS!"

Will was still reeling from the slap when he felt a pair of arms circling around his chest from behind, while someone else forcefully unbuckled his belt and yanked down his pants and underwear.

Will's father first explained the reason for not having him and his brother circumcised when they began asking him at an early age how come their penises were different from the other kids. "Because that's how God made you and that's how you were meant to be!" When they got a little older, their Dad offered the more Darwinian explanation that humans evolved with foreskins because the penis is a sensitive organ that requires protection. "Who are we," he argued, "to tamper with hundreds of thousands years of evolution?"

With Will now on display, the men in the room slowly broke into a chorus of "I'll be damneds" and variations on that theme, before turning on Donny. They no longer hesitated to call him by his name either. "So much for your Jew-boy, Donny!" laughed one of them. Another whooped, "I remember when we used to go skinny- dipping, Donny! Maybe you're the Jew-boy!" With Will still standing there drop-trou-shriveled in the midst of all that whoopin' and hollerin'.

Donny was humiliated by his "mistaken-identity" blunder. He was also furious that his cover was blown and in a panic, cried out, "Who's *Donny*? There's no *Donny* here!"

It was a scene of utter bedlam.

Finally, the boss-man intervened yet again, and order was re-established if you didn't count some snickering still hanging in the air. Will took advantage of the lull to request that his pants be pulled up. Smith assigned Donny to the task. "Son, now you go and lift up Mr. Kraft's trousers, you damned fool!"

Still smarting from all the verbal abuse, Donny lashed out. "You can't blame me for something my parents done to me when I was a baby," he whined. "That was their doing, not mine!" Donny paused momentarily. In desperation, he yelled out the common challenge that the men could all go and perform an anatomically impossible act, which served only to invite further ridicule.

"At least we'll be doing it with intact dicks," quipped Jimmy -crack- corn.

The ribbing Donny was subjected to had been merciless. Even Will experienced a tinge of *Schadenfreude*. Just a little.

But Smith had now had enough. "All of you, shut up!" he demanded. "Stop with this ridiculousness!" There was a long pause while he looked sternly at his men.

"Donny, show Mr.Kraft back to his private room."

Once again, Will was quickly hog-tied and dragged back to the adjoining room with its cold concrete floor. Just to escape the scorn being heaped upon him, Donny decided to stay in the room with Will. During this brief interval, Will devised what could be called a "got-nothing-to-lose" strategy, picking up on Donny's earlier comment about resenting his parents' decision to have him circumcised.

"Donny! Donny, I know it's you!" Will whispered.

"What the hell you mean 'I know it's you'? You don't know me. There's plenty guys named Donny."

"OK then. Maybe you're not the Donny I was thinking of," Will conceded. "No matter… you're still a circumcised Donny, and I'm trying to help you here!" Now feigning sympathy, Will was going to offer Donny some advice. He lowered his voice to a whisper. "Donny, you don't have to stay circumcised, you know. You can get yourself '*re-uncircumcised*'. Doctors now have a way of putting a foreskin back on your dick. You've heard of organ donations?"

"That's for kidneys and stuff…"

"…and foreskins!"

"Foreskins?"

"That's what I'm trying to tell you, Donny! And lower your voice. I don't want them hearing this conversation in the other room. They might think we're gay or something. But yes, Donny…foreskins! You see, there are lots of healthy young men that die in the prime of life. Fortunately, many of them signed up to be organ donors. That's livers, kidneys, hearts, and yes…foreskins! So Aryans like yourself really don't have to live out their entire lives with a dick not of their own choosing."

"So what exactly is it you're trying to tell me?" asked a suddenly, very interested Donny.

"I'm saying that thanks to organ-donating young men, some of whom died while exercising their civil liberty of riding a motorcycle uncircumcised—and without a helmet—there's an abundance of foreskins waiting to be harvested for unfortunate guys like yourself. I should say like with any organ, you'd have to find the right match, and there's a slight risk of rejection, but…"

Excitedly, Donny interrupted, "Where can you get that operation done? Here in Montana?"

"Of course not! Here in Montana, the Aryans are so perfect, that plastic surgeons would go out of business. You gotta go to CALIFORNIA!" Will enunciated *California* real dreamy and theatrical, like the place The Mamas and the Papas sang about, and not just a state run by an Austrian body-builder- governor. "They do everything there," Will assured, "boobs, noses, buttocks, pecs and yes…dicks!"

Donny had a few more questions. Then he closed the door behind him and re-entered the main room where Smith and his minions were still discussing strategy. With much bravado he announced, "Boss, you don't need to worry about Kraft. I left him so scared in there, I think he may have shit himself!"

"Right, Donny," growled Smith. "Now do us all a favor and go the hell home!"

"Sure, boss!" Donny replied cheerfully. "If you need me, you know where to find me."

Even as those words quivered out of his mouth, Donny was making travel plans. To California. Donny sensed that Smith was not happy with him. He also knew that folks who made Smith unhappy had a way of disappearing. As it turned out, Donny's concerns were justified. While Donny was making his plans, Tillman Smith was indeed making plans of his own for this weak-link-turned-liability.

CHAPTER 21

THE ESCAPE

Will was once again alone, back in the room with the concrete floor. At least he thought he was alone. His wrists were tied to his ankles even tighter than before. Apparently, Donny was gone, but he wondered if they had left anyone else to watch over him. Remaining still for a few minutes, he hoped to calm his nerves while listening for movement, breathing...anything. Finally, he was satisfied no one else was in the room.

He wriggled across the concrete floor until until reaching a wall. He feared that his back or hamstrings would cramp up...then what? By working his way along the wall, he estimated the room to be about ten by ten and empty, possibly an unused storage area. But what about surveillance cameras? What if they were laughing at his clumsy movements right now? Will chose to assume they were not.

While working his way along the wall, Will became aware of type of baseboard heating unit similar to the type used in his house back home. From experience repairing and cleaning them, he knew that removing the endcap exposed some rather sharp edges. Could those edges serve to cut through the plastic ties used to restrain him? Would he have enough time? And if he did free himself, then what?

These thoughts raced through his mind along with another very dark possibility. What if they re-entered the room and caught him in the act? And then an even darker one. What if he didn't make an escape attempt, desperate as it was, and his captors decided do away with him? Would he go out in a burst of self-recrimination over his indecisiveness? Would groveling in self -reproach be his final living performance?

Sliding his back up against the wall, Will ran his hands over an endcap. They always seemed to pop off easily, but of course that was with eyes wide open and hands free. He positioned himself as best as he could, then clasped what felt like the endcap, wrapped his fingernails as tightly as possible around the edges, and struggled to pry off the piece. He gave it a hard tug. Nothing! Regrouping, he tried again. This time, by pulling in an upward direction, he finally had success! Holding the part in his fingers, he gently placed it on the floor, and slid it out of the way. Not easy with shaking hands.

Will then probed the newly exposed edges, almost slicing his fingers in the process. His first goal was to sever the tie between the wrists and ankles, the one that had him hogtied! Maneuvering the plastic tie against the sharp metal, he began a sawing motion. It seemed to take forever but finally his hands and feet were separated.

Everything in fact seemed to be taking forever. He had no way of knowing how much time had passed. More critical, however, was how much time he had left. How could he possibly know. Was it seconds, minutes... hours?

Will lifted his blindfold. Light seeping in through the window from the exterior allowed him to see, if only a little. He then began sawing away at the wrist tie, which he finally severed. Once again, it seemed to take forever. Lastly, he cut the ankle restraints. His limbs were free!

He scanned the room. No video cameras, that he could see anyway. Going to the large double-hung window, Will Gently separated the blinds and looked outside. Some pickup trucks were parked in the driveway next to an enormous three car garage. A full moon illuminated a distant ridge. He would have to act quickly!

While cutting his bindings, Will had been able to pick up pieces of conversation taking place in the neighboring room. "Of course it's kidnapping!" someone had confirmed. And then another voice, "... not until we ask for a ransom..." Then, "You don't know what you're talking about," and a protesting "... no choice in the matter now!" After a brief silence, someone pointed out, "No one even knows he's missing yet!" They were continuing the argument about how to deal with him. Most ominous was the remark about "being judged by history" which he thought he heard several times.

Passively awaiting their decision was not an option. He had already taken the first step by severing the zip-ties. There was no turning around.

Will quickly examined the window. Was there a home security system… motion detection sensors? If so, he was hopeful that the system had been disarmed. But what if it was one of those sophisticated types that remained in operation even when the house was occupied? He refused to accept that possibility.

Time to get out of here! Will cautiously clicked open the two latches, lifting the heavy lower pane. He swung his left leg out, briefly straddling the windowsill before backing his other leg out, then gently lowered himself into the soft mulch along the edge.

Exterior floodlights required him to make his way furtively along the shadows, crouched, animal-like. There was one especially troublesome bright patch that he had to scamper across as light-footed as possible before ducking under the rear of a mud-caked pickup. His heart was racing. From his crouched position, Will glanced up into the truck bed. There, to his astonishment, was his backpack and walking stick! He reached in and snatched them, a reflex more than a decision, and dashed off into the darkness. Hidden behind the garage, will paused once again and looked back. He could see the lit room where the men were still arguing. The small room in which he had been held captive remained dark. He turned and sprinted into the forest.

Back in the cabin, the debate over Will's fate continued, at times heatedly. One Front member who had briefly been a pre law major at the University of Montana, argued that even if they were to voluntarily release their captive, members would still be subject to felony charges. Worse yet would be the exposure of The Front's operations and membership roster.

For all his bad-ass looks, Aaron Barber had been quite persuasive in his argument to release Will. They could explain to him that there had been a misunderstanding on the part of the low IQ tormentor, Donny Jackson. "Give me a chance to reason with Kraft," Barber pleaded. "I'll convince him that what we have here is nothing more than a 'no harm- no foul' situation. Maybe provide some incentives, sweeten the pot sort to speak, and get him to drop the whole unfortunate matter."

After further discussion and refinement, Barber's strategy was adopted. They came up with a proposal for Will. They would describe it as a "win-win," but at the same time make it clear that rejecting the proposal would be unwise, maybe even foolhardy. Tillman Smith would do the explaining.

"OK then. Aaron, you go in there, untie Kraft and bring him back in here. But first let me summarize. Are you guys listening?" Smith waited for everyone's attention. "It will be explained that an unfortunate misunderstanding had taken place. In recognition of the error, we have a proposal that should certainly be amenable to 'all the parties involved'. One that will allow us to go forward amicably and in the spirit of brotherhood…"

"…I think that 'brotherhood' thing is important," interjected one of the men.

"Let me finish… UNINTERRUPTED," Smith snapped back, "then anyone can say what they have to say!" He continued. "I will also explain that Donny, due to his intellectual limitations, had made a serious error in judgment, and will be severely disciplined."

He then went on with the details of their "sweetened pot." In return for his cooperation to help resolve the misunderstanding, Will would be offered an all-expense paid, ten day guided elk hunt this October in The Bob: the same deluxe package for which wealthy clients from California paid handsomely. In the event that his personal calendar precluded such a once-in-a-lifetime adventure, a cash equivalent would be offered instead.

"And when Mr. Kraft is brought back into the room," Smith raised his voice, "I will do the talking! Not a word out of any of you. Is that clear?"

Trying to be helpful, one of the men advised "Yeah! And make sure to really build it up…like how they do it on 'The Price is Right'!"

Smith glared at him. He shut up immediately.

"OK, Aaron," Smith instructed. "Now go in there and untie Mr. Kraft, and bring him back in here. As gently as possible."

Barber got out of his chair and walked to the room. He opened the door slowly and turned on the light. For a few seconds he stared in disbelief. The room was empty and the window was wide open. Then he turned around and looked at the men, "Boys, I believe we got a little problem on our hands!"

CHAPTER 22

FINALLY FREE!

—◦◦◦—

Desperate to put distance between himself and his captors, Will recklessly ran, crawled and climbed hand over foot, stumbling and falling. His hands and knees were scraped and bloodied. That he hadn't broken a bone or sprained an ankle was in itself miraculous.

His flight from hell was a heart pumping, lung burning, uphill, burst of energy. A half hour later, he stood atop a cliff with a partial view of the cabin below. Leaning against a gnarled Ponderosa and gasping for breath, he could make out the commotion unfolding around the lodge where just a short time ago he had been held captive. It was a frantic scene. Powerful flashlight and headlight beams were scanning in all directions. So far at least, it appeared that they had no idea in what direction he had escaped.

Will could hear a megaphone amplified voice beseeching, **"You are making a mistake! Come back and talk to us! We can work things out... there's been a mistake! Come back, talk to us! You're only making it worse for yourself!"**

After a few minutes he had recovered sufficiently to continue his ascent into the high country, his refuge.

Hours later he found himself walking across an expansive alpine meadow under the full moon. His stride had slowed considerably. It was no longer frantic. Still, he maintained a metronome pace in a direction up the mountain and away from his nightmare. Once he did come upon a well used trail but got off immediately. He couldn't take the risk.

A clear moonlit night. It was an opportunity to go through the wilderness unaided by flashlight, especially out in the open as he was now. But it worked both ways. He could also be spotted easily. He suddenly felt vulnerable, and chose a path parallel to a noisy willow -choked rivulet, far enough away so he could still hear pursuers, but close enough for him to duck into hiding if necessary. Grizzlies roamed these mountains…the apex predator… but they were the least of his concerns.

Will's watch read 1AM. He had been on the run for at least four hours maybe five. He was physically spent. Thirst is rarely a problem in the Northern Rockies with its many ribbons of pristine water. Fear, however, and extreme exertion can bring about dehydration rapidly. He had to remind himself to drink water at every opportunity.

Discovering his backpack in the pickup was a stroke of luck. Upon finding it, he had mumbled some words of thanks for his captors' carelessness, or was it stupidity? No matter, it was once again in his possession filled with the necessities for his adventure, the seven day hike that he had planned into the Bob Marshall Wilderness Complex. Now the backpack meant survival. "The Bob" as it was known reverently to trekkers, was the most remote wild area in the lower forty eight. Will had rambled through its vastness on several previous occasions, with his about-to-be ex-wife, his friends and even his children. Those previous excursions, filled with awe and wonderment, held fond memories for him. Although the trips were physically demanding, Will had always managed to set a pace that allowed ample time to observe the scenery and wildlife, to fly fish for native Cutthroat Trout and capture memories through his camera lens. Now it was different. He was a hunted person. Though elated by his new-found freedom, he was terrified that it would be short-lived.

The first few hours of his flight had been fueled by adrenalin. Now he could sense that collapse from physical exhaustion was entirely possible. His legs were heavy, causing him to stumble with greater frequency. Breathing was becoming difficult and the elevation made it worse. He was also becoming careless, perhaps even reckless. Several times he ran into low hanging branches. What if he injured an eye?

There was also the abiding concern that his pursuers would soon track him down. Some of them were experienced outdoorsmen, probably hunters. What if they had lion dogs like Blue Ticks or Black and Tans that could easily pick up his now pungent scent? At one point Will came upon a sizable creek. Willing to risk a fall on the slick boulders in order to throw off the dogs, he gripped his hiking stick tightly and stepped into the water and carefully sloshed his way upstream. The stick always came with him on his treks, and held special meaning for Will. A few years ago, his son had fashioned it out of a piece of sassafras and presented it to him as a Father's Day gift. Since that time it had become a real beauty, polyurethaned and gussied up with emblems collected from the many national parks and forests they had visited. Stout and about seven feet in length, it could handle the pushing-off forces of steep ascents, or when applying the brakes on descent. It came in especially handy during this treacherous aquatic detour.

Traveling wilderness trails requires fitness. Going off the trails, bushwhacking, especially through thick forests, was virtually impossible, even for someone in top physical condition. It meant encountering encountering obstacles like large boulders and fallen trees, treading on ground where no human before had gone. On the other hand, staying too long on established trails carried the risk of being recaptured by his pursuers. Another problem at the moment was that he really had no idea where he was. Yes, somewhere in The Bob…that much he knew. He also knew that he was now in high elevation. Beyond that, he couldn't say for sure.

It was probably already close to sunrise when he was crossing a high alpine meadow. Along its edge, he could make out a small copse of spruce trees nestled at the base of a large granite outcrop: under normal conditions, not a place he would choose for a campsite, away from any lake or creek as it was. But his quads were starting to quiver during the slightest of ascents and descents were no better. He had the gracefulness of a drunk at closing time. He made his way to the grove. He could go no further.

Will unpacked his foam roller and sleeping bag. That would be all. No campfire. No tent. No cooked meal. He collapsed. It was a state of exhaustion beyond anything he had ever experienced. Not in his entire life.

The full moon and blanket of sparkling stars provided a few seconds of ecstasy. Then, nothing.

CHAPTER 23

IN THE WILDERNESS

———— Ɡ ————

When he finally came to, it was close to five in the afternoon. He had slept almost twelve hours, and if not for the raucous cry of the grey jay perched above him, he would have slept longer. These birds were notorious camp robbers, and this particular one was scolding Will for his impertinence. How dare he not leave food scraps!

Groggy and disoriented, it took a few seconds for Will to recall his circumstances. He rubbed his eyes and looked around. Rays of afternoon sunlight penetrated the boughs above. Already halfway out of his sleeping bag, he noted that the air was surprisingly warm. Slowly, he slid out of his down cocoon. Every muscle in his body ached.

Will felt a burning sensation in his palms. He looked down and saw that they were scratched, blistered and filthy. His left pant leg was torn revealing a badly bruised knee. His shirt, the com-fort-ably-love-ly one, was tattered beyond repair.

Looking around, nothing seemed familiar. Of course. He had arrived here in the darkness: things always look different in daylight. Still, he was a bit surprised at the scantiness of the stand of trees he had chosen as his refuge, but was that really a choice or simply the inability to take another step?

He emerged from seclusion, slowly, and in a few steps stood before an expansive alpine meadow. The sun's brightness forced him to shade his eyes and squint. First he scanned his surroundings to make sure that he was in fact alone. He saw nothing to raise an alarm and heard only the trilling of nearby songbirds and the croaking of a distant raven.

In last night's darkness, despite the full moon, he hadn't seen anything that resembled the breathtaking scene now in front of him. Spring comes late to alpine meadows, but when it arrives, they are transformed into a kaleidoscope of color. He was able to identify the vibrant red Indian Paintbrushes and the cobalt blue Gentians. Dramatic white clusters atop of long stalks punctuated the fields; beargrass! And so much more. Nuances of red and blue as well as yellow, rose, purple… maybe the entire color wheel filled the verdant vista. The uncommon beauty was electrifying. Soon, he allowed himself to surrender to the moment and stood there in a zen-like trance

It was a full half hour before he stepped back into the asylum of the grove to sit on the trunk of a fallen tree. His thoughts turned to more practical matters. For one thing, he realized that he himself reeked of that odor peculiar to those whose physical exertion has been augmented by fear. More than a trace had permeated the lining of his bag. It would need to be aired out. While at it, he thought about finding the nearest creek and tend to his personal hygiene situation, then immediately recognized the absurdity of that notion. *To what end?* So for the moment, he simply sat on the deadfall and attempted to reconstruct the last few days.

His thoughts went back to the hotel in downtown Missoula where he had spent the night and his early start the following day. He recalled the friendly folks that had gotten him up to Choteau, the couple from Wisconsin and that talkative young fellow, Liam Johnson. There was Hal Miller, the "Hoot", and that warm reception Will had received at the colony. Things had gotten off to such a great start here in Montana. How did they go so terribly wrong?

Seated on the fallen tree, Will continued surveilling his surroundings. He needed to get back to practical matters. For starters, where the hell was he? Will unfolded a topo map and laid it out in front of him. The map was not overly informative. But for the moment at least, it was reassuring to know that he was far away from the nearest marked trail. Away from people. He retrieved his binoculars and climbed to the top of the outcrop above him for a better look. He saw no humans and no evidence of them, such as campfire smoke. In addition, there was no evidence of foul weather, confirming the forecast he had heard a few days back in Missoula.

Still looking through the binocs, he caught sight of a golden eagle below him, soaring the thermals. The singularity of his vantage point, actually looking down on the raptor, was not lost on him. It became a memory that would remain with him forever. How is it that fleeting moments like this leave such outsized impressions? It also occurred to him that he may have been the only human to have ever sat upon that promontory. It was a thought he cherished.

Then his imagination took another turn as he began conjuring up a host of "what-if" scenarios. *What if* he had decided to stay in Missoula for another night or two? After all, he had always enjoyed the city for its western ambience and friendly college town atmosphere. *What if* he had heeded that hokey sign at the Jackelope about discussing politics at your own risk, and did he really need such a sign to remind him? Hadn't Annie already advised him to try filtering his remarks? *What if* he had simply gone right to bed in his "less-smoking" room at the Trail's End, or had simply left the bar after a burger and beer?

Someone once said, "An adventure is what happens when you screw up." Possibly true, thought Will, but it's only an adventure if you survive. If you don't, it's stupidity.

It was also possible that none of those "what-ifs" would have made a difference. Maybe it was in his DNA. Maybe he inherited some sort of "victim" gene. After all, he became a victim of his wife's idiosyncrasies… or were they his? He had also become the victim in the clash between his nonconformist teaching style and the dictatorial demands of the school's administration.

Perhaps for no reason other than he was who he was, did he now find himself in this predicament. Not a simple twist of fate, or bad luck, but something predetermined, as in the words of the old Blues standard,

If it weren't for bad luck,
I wouldn't have no luck at all.

If it hadn't been this crazy thing between him and The Front, it would have been something else. or so he had convinced himself. Alone with his thoughts, they had taken a dark turn. Maybe he needed a distraction. And then at that very moment, one came.

Out of the corner of his eye, he caught something flying into a fir tree only fifty or sixty feet away, something fairly large. Through his binoculars, he scanned the boughs for a few moments and spotted a large round bird; a spruce grouse was perched in a lower branch perhaps ten feet off the ground. Though related to the eastern roughed grouse, these western cousins behaved quite differently. Relying on camouflage, they will often sat still, allowing humans to approach quite closely. Early explorers dubbed them "fool-hens". Will wasn't going to pass up the opportunity.

Reaching into his backpack, he pulled out his Wrist-Rocket slingshot, inserted a steel ball into the pouch. He slowly approached the fowl. Forty feet...thirty. At about twenty feet, Will took aim and released the projectile. A soft thud followed and an explosion of feathers, and the bird half fell – half fluttered to the ground. Dinner!

After plucking its feathers, He carved the bird into parts and sprinkled them with a mix of flour, salt, pepper and tarragon. The small stove already lit, he placed a dollop of Crisco into the pan and when hot enough, placed the bird parts in, turning them a few time until brown all around. Finally, he added a dash of brandy (it always came along when backpacking) to deglaze, and *voila!* He was enjoying a most delectable wildfowl banquet.

For the first time in days, Will was able to relax. He pitched his small tent and crawled inside. He always brought a book to read on his adventures, typically something regional that enhanced his sense of place. He reached into his backpack for Nothing But Blue Skies, the McGuane paperback he had purchased back in Missoula.

Temperatures began to drop. He put on a fleece, crawled into his sleeping bag and managed to read a few chapters. It was always surprising for Will how late it was in this part of Montana before getting dark. But it wasn't loss of daylight that made him put the book down. Off in the distance came the sound of a wolf pack. It began with an indistinct series of yips and barks, then erupted into a lugubrious full-throated chorus before descending back down to a satisfied repose.

A proper welcome to the wilderness.

CHAPTER 24

WILL NEEDS A PLAN

———cℕɔ———

Exhilarating as it was, simply escaping the clutches of The Front did not constitute a plan of action.

It was said that Moses, leading the Jews out of Egypt, would constantly remind them, "It ain't over til it's over!" He thought the words had an inspirational ring to them.

"But that's not a PLAN!" shot back the Hebrews.

So even Moses had to come up with a plan to reach The Promised Land.

Will had yet to come up with his own plan. He wasn't even sure what his own *promised land* was. The only thing he knew for certain was that unlike Moses, he couldn't rely on divine intervention to get him there. These thoughts were racing through his mind while finishing breakfast the following day. Then an even more disturbing thought occurred to him.

Will had convinced himself that the Front had already launched a massive search operation. At this very moment, he speculated, groups were driving up and down the highways along the Front and the less used logging roads as well. The Bob itself was being combed by men on horseback. He gave them a name; *Searchers*.

The Searchers would be asking trekkers, backpackers, outfitters and whomever they came across, if they had encountered a lone white male, about forty years old, average height, maybe bearded, maybe with a New York accent. If so, they would warn, be careful! A fellow fitting that description was on the run after ravaging an innocent blond cheerleader... or was it a Boy Scout... and he was considered dangerous and desperate. He needed to be apprehended before he escaped back to Sodom or was it Gomorrah...or maybe New York City? And oh... a considerable reward awaits the person who could assist in his capture.

In Will's scenario, "wanted" posters had been tacked up on utility poles throughout this part of the state. The posters would warn folks to not pick up hitchhikers and to make sure that their cars and houses were locked. Residents would be instructed to remind their children to not go out alone, especially at night, that the man in question was a known pederast. (Many of the locals would have to search through dictionaries for the meaning of that word...) There would be a hotline number and people would be cautioned not to confront the man unless they were armed.

As is the case with any rumor, few would go through the trouble of fact-checking. The notoriety of the subject's heinous deeds would indeed, grow by the hour. *Pity the average height- white male who innocently wandered into this part of Montana at this time* thought Will.

Will pondered his present situation of being alone in the vastness of The Bob. If Searchers did come upon him, the result would be summary execution, his body left to be scavenged by bears and wolves. All people would ever know is that he foolishly embarked upon a solo backpacking trip into The Bob and was never seen again, maybe killed by a grizzly. No one would ever suspect...foul play!

To remain out of sight would be his strategy. No contact with anyone: not with backpackers, not with fishermen and not with outfitter led groups. Not even with Forest Service employees and trail maintenance crews. No one could be trusted. He would stay away from the marked trails, especially well-used ones, and avoid established campsites. He would confine his escape route to the upper elevations as much as possible, the high country that rarely saw humans. The Bob's vastness would protect him. Still, never-ending vigilance would be necessary. After all, any person he encountered, even an outfitter or wrangler not involved with The Front, would see it as his duty to turn in this known rapist, especially with a monetary reward waiting. A moment of carelessness or misplaced trust was all that it would take.

But remain undetected to what end? There had to be a safe haven somewhere, and he had to figure out where that would be. In the meantime, he would remain unseen.

As far as his family was concerned, and anyone else that knew him, Will was not *missing*. Not for the next few weeks at least. People knew that he needed to "get away" and was seeking solace in the Montana wilderness: a place where the "earth and its community are untrammeled by man" (those words directly from The Wilderness Act passed back in 1964). Will wouldn't be reported *missing* —not for a while at least—since this was a self-imposed exile. So the fact that he wouldn't be heard from for a while was no cause for alarm. If anything, that was the plan! As for why his name didn't appear at any of those sign-in boxes placed at trailheads? Probably just an oversight on Will's part...

Back in 1984, a twenty two year old Olympic biathlete named Kari Swenson went for a training run on a mountain trail near her home in Big Sky, Montana. On her run, she accidentally encountered two self-proclaimed "survivalists", fifty two year old Don Nichols and his nineteen year old son, Dan. Their plan to kidnap a woman for "companionship" had apparently already been hatched. Swenson was in the wrong place at the right time.

A rescue was attempted by two friends, Allan Goldstein and Jim Schwalbe. In the end, Swenson was accidentally wounded and Goldstein fatally shot. Fortunately, Schwalbe was able to run for help.

The Nichols left the wounded Swenson behind and fled into the mountains. Despite a search effort involving a SWAT Team, FBI agents with night vision goggles and heat sensors as well as private trackers with dogs, the so-called "mountain men" vanished. They managed to elude capture for five months before being discovered in a secluded campsite in the wilderness not far from Bozeman, Montana.

Will remembered the incident well. The thought occurred to him that if those two miscreants could remain hidden in the wilds for five months despite a sophisticated search effort, he should have no problem keeping out of sight for a shorter period of time until reaching a safe haven.

But he had yet to figure out where that safe haven would be. He needed a place to re-enter *civilization* and report his ordeal to authorities without alerting sympathizers to The Front. He had convinced himself that locals would believe that a dangerous man fitting his description was on the loose. Furthermore, the idea of reaching out to the local constabulary was a chance he couldn't take. Didn't law enforcement folks often get quite chummy with the locals, especially with charismatic types like Tillman Smith, head honcho of The Front?

After considering his options, Will narrowed them down to two. One was to head north and exit the Wilderness where it borders Glacier National Park. The other was head more west and make his way to The Swan Valley. The chance that folks that far away would have any connection with The Front was unlikely. But what if these white supremacist groups were all part of a bigger network? What if they were all connected and in communication with one another?

He decided to move in a northwesterly direction and thereby continue to put more distance between him and his pursuers. He would go deeper into the wilderness. The further he went, he reasoned, the less the risk of falling back into the hands of The Front or their sympathizers.

CHAPTER 25

STILL IN THE
WILDERNESS

——◦◊◦——

I'm sorry for the way things turned out between us, Katie, and I'm not sure in what direction we're going, but right now those issues will have to be put aside because you and the kids may be in grave danger.

Or perhaps it would sound less alarming if he simply said, *Katie, you haven't heard from me in a while. I ran into a little problem out here in Montana, so give me a few minutes to explain...*

Will found himself rehearsing the best way to explain his situation to Katie once he got out of The Bob. But the whole thing sounded so preposterous that he decided that perhaps informing Katie would best be left to the *authorities,* whoever that might be.

As for making his way out of The Bob, he was on the right path. Or at least he thought so. According to his topo map, he was heading in a direction that would eventually take him to a major trail which would in turn lead him to a trailhead near Rte.2, the border between Glacier National Park and the Bob Marshall Wilderness complex. There, he would be approximately eighty miles from Choteau. Far enough away from The Front, he calculated, but close enough to *civilization* to make a phone call to...who exactly would he call?

No matter what, he would have to leave the wilderness. For now at least, he would continue to stay up in the higher elevations and on little used trails. Main trails through The Bob, though remote, still saw occasional human traffic. Eventually, he would be on such a trail. He reassured himself that the likelihood of an encounter with members of The Front or their sympathizers was highly unlikely. *But it remained a possibility.*

A few hours ago and a thousand feet higher, Will had traversed a large snowfield that remained locked in the shadows. Though his footprints remained, in a matter of a few weeks they would be gone. Still, Will wondered if leaving those footprints had been a mistake. Was he was being overly paranoid? Not for the first time that humorous quip... was it Woody Allen? *Even paranoids are right some of the time,* came to mind. Under the circumstances, could he be blamed?

Hundreds... no thousands of nature lovers, adventure seekers and sportsmen entered the Montana wilderness every year to enjoy the scenery, to see wildlife and catch fish. They return home with lasting memories, joyful memories. Will still couldn't believe that he had gotten himself into this mess.

Although he no longer wallowed in self-recrimination like the day before, Will still found himself in a bit of a funk. He had to snap out of it. *Shit happens,* after all. Simply living life entails a certain amount of risk. One didn't have to be an actuarial to know that. There's always the probability of a fatal car accident or becoming the victim of a crime through no fault of your own. There is such a thing as fate. Maybe that eminent philosopher, Dr. John, summed it all up when he mused,

> *I been in the right place but it must have been*
> *the wrong time*
> *I'd have said the right thing*
> *But I must have used the wrong line...*

Tending to more practical matters, Will checked his topo map. According to that map, he was close to 7'000 feet in elevation. If he kept the present course, a gradual descent would eventually bring him down to about 4,000 feet. As he slowly descended from the higher elevations, the carpets of colorful alpine flora began to change into a more uniform green. Winter's melting snowpack trickled into the creeks and rivers below. Yesterday the waters flowed into the mighty Missouri, the Mississippi and into the Gulf of Mexico. Today it was all destined for the Pacific. When he eventually left the wilderness, he would be in another valley or as they said in the West, another *drainage.*

The important thing for now was that with each step, Will was putting distance between himself and The Front.

He glanced down at his watch. About five hours of daylight remained. Eventually, he would have to find a suitable place to pitch his tent, his third night in the wilderness. *Suitable* meaning away from the trail…out of sight… certainly not in one of the established campsites that dotted the wilderness. He was feeling a little more relaxed. Less on the run. He wondered if he'd be able to recapture the sense of unbridled pleasure he always experienced on previous backpacking adventures? At the moment, it felt unlikely.

As Will rounded a large outcrop, movement in a distant meadow caught his attention. He came to a halt and reached for his binoculars. He couldn't believe his eyes: a large grizzly bear with two cubs was busy dismantling a large rotting log. Mama was doing all the work. While she pawed through the log, her youngsters engaged in play wrestling with occasional short bursts up the nearby stumps. That the bears were upwind from him was a good thing. Nonetheless, Will scanned his immediate surroundings. Even though the Bruin family was over a thousand feet away, he was looking for a tree to climb, should mother grizz decide to come his way.

Will had always been told that unlike their black bear cousins, adult grizzlies didn't climb trees. He took note of an old Engelmann Spruce behind him. With its low stout branches, he knew that if he had to, he could climb it. Only later would he learn that the 'grizzlies don't climb trees' thing was a myth. Ignorance is bliss.

Will dropped his backpack and slowly backed up a few feet to position himself behind a large boulder. From there he would continue to observe the bears for the next hour. Every so often, Mama would take a break from foraging and stand upright to sniff the air. She stood almost 7 feet. Will was able to get a good look at the "dished" face and prominent shoulder hump that left no doubt that this was *Ursus arctos horribilis* and not it's smaller cousin, *Ursus americanus.* Many so-called black bears in the West are actually brown or cinnamon in color, but this one was definitely a "grizz".

During their legendary Voyage of Discovery, Lewis and Clark first observed the grizzly in what is now South Dakota. The explorers would have many more encounters throughout their journey. The following anthropomorphic account appears in Lewis' journal: "I must confess that I do not like the 'gentlemen' and had rather fight two Indians than one bear."

In another journal entry, Lewis observed that the beast was "extreemly hard to kill." Clark added that it was "…verry large and a turrible looking animal." [sic]

Grizzly bear attacks have continued into the 21st Century, and of course, Will knew this. But he also knew that such attacks were extremely rare. He also recognized that at the moment he still had greater concerns than a mother grizz with cubs. He stood still and observed for another half hour. The clowning of the cubs was especially comical. When was the last time he actually laughed? It was just the distraction he needed.

After the bear encounter, Will continued his slow descent. At one point while making his way through acres of talus, pikas began popping up from behind boulders and diving back into their burrows with high-pitched alarm calls. Again, he took time to watch their antics, which at times resembled a "Whack-a-Mole" performance. Although fascinating…and entertaining, they were no match for the bears: the *charismatic megafauna.*

Almost immediately after the pikas, the path, nothing more than a game trail of sorts, took him under a steep cliff. Once again, something caught Will's eye. Pausing to look up, he spotted a family of Rocky Mountain Goats. He reached again for his binoculars through which he counted seven, including two small kids. Will looked on in astonishment. How they managed to secure purchase on their meager pathway seemed extraordinary. That reputation for sure-footedness was well deserved. Their presence also served to remind him that he was still in higher elevations and had a ways to go before reaching the river below and the main trail.

As Will continued down the game trail, it widened, making progress easier. A few hours later, he entered an expansive "burn", where years earlier a fire had raged. This had been a great conflagration indeed. Over time, the remnants of dead trees had become weathered, bleached totems: monuments to the destructive forces of nature. It was a frightening, yet majestic landscape. An endless carpet of fireweed had colonized the forest floor and the profusion of pink-magenta blossoms intensified the ghost-like appearance of the trunks. Scattered amongst the fireweed, young conifers reached upward: the forest of the future. In hundreds of years, any evidence of the fire will have vanished. *Resurrection and rebirth.*

He paused to photograph his surroundings, and write down his thoughts. The fact that he was now taking time to chronicle his experience meant that he had crossed a threshold of sorts. In his notes he speculated on how long ago it had been since the inferno had swept through. He surmised five or at most ten years. During the respite, Will took out his canteen and gleefully consumed half of it. It was early summer, and he was thankful for the abundance of clean, fresh water in the Northern Rockies.

A while later, he came to a small creek. The creek's water had certainly been well filtered by the miles of stone and gravel through which it travelled. Some backpackers always boiled their water or ran it through specially made filters to screen out the parasite *Giardia lamblia,* which if ingested, can wreak G.I. havoc. He certainly didn't need diarrhea to add to his woes. But by choosing his water sources carefully, Will had never been afflicted. He held his canteen gently under the gin-clear flow.

While refilling, he heard a buzzing sound above his head. Looking up, he saw a hummingbird with a brilliant, iridescent orange-red throat. Where had he read that the bird symbolizes lightness of being and enjoyment of life. It was also said to embody the quality of resiliency? A truly remarkable little thing, it could travel great distances effortlessly and was the only bird able to fly backwards. Native Americans viewed these feathered jewels as bringers of good fortune. Will eagerly grasped on to the significance of the bird's visit. He wasn't looking for another omen, but recognized one when he saw it.

He would continue on his way with a newly discovered lightness in his steps.

CHAPTER 26

ONE FOOT IN FRONT OF THE OTHER

Trekkers are advised to carry backpacks no heavier than 20% of their body weight and Will had always paid scrupulous attention to that recommendation. Though he started out with 38 lbs, his body weight had surely fallen well below 190 over the the last several days. But when you are struggling on an upward ascent, the contour lines of the topo map tightly bunched, it would be reasonable to question the validity of that 20% rule. In fact, it would be reasonable to question the sanity of backpacking itself.

As a distraction, he toyed with some mathematical calculations. One involved length of stride and number of steps per minute to determine miles covered each hour, and the distance he could expect to cover over the course of a day. Take the portion of trail over which he now struggled, for example. Will estimated that by maintaining his present stride, his rate of progress was well under a mile per hour. Fortunately for him, contour lines weren't always this tightly compressed, and for every ascent there was a downhill.

Those steep declines by the way, though reducing cardiovascular demand, were oh so tough in the knees! That's where the IB Profin came in handy. Applying the brakes with his beloved sassafras hiking stick helped as well.

Another calculation with which Will liked to play, was figuring out the rise, run and slope of the trails. By applying algebra concepts learned back in high school, he kept himself focused on things other than the physical torment he Now was undergoing. Fun as these mental gymnastics were, it still came down to one inescapable fact: you make progress by putting one foot in front of the other.

Nocturnal trekking could also be added to his accomplishments. Will had made the decision to travel into the night, and the clear sky and still substantial waning gibbous moon helped. Though he had a flashlight, it was rarely turned on, thereby allowing his rods and cones to fully adapt to the darkness. Although he was still a diurnal creature out of its element, nighttime travel did allow him to get back on some of the main trails. Here, he would make better progress.

It did occur to Will that some serious predators were also more active at night, and that the possibility of an encounter with a mountain lion, or perhaps a bear or wolf might be greater. But the human, the true apex predator, was diurnal, and that was the one he feared the most.

He thought about how he would react in the unlikely scenario of an encounter with horseback riders or backpackers. *What if they were searchers?* What if they had been placed by the trailheads, lurking in the shadows waiting for Will? Of course, he still had no idea if Searchers even existed, but dismissing the idea would have been foolhardy indeed.

Temperatures drop considerably at night in the Northern Rockies, even during early summer. Will removed a light fleece from his backpack after the sun set, Lower temperatures meant that he was sweating less. Even on strenuous parts of the trail, fewer water breaks were required, and his energy level remained higher. By now, Will pretty much knew his exact location in The Bob, thanks to some rustic trail signs posted by the Forest Service. On the other hand, the darkness increased the risk of becoming completely lost. Still, *One foot in front of the other.*

Will reckoned that there would be one more night in the wilderness. Barring any unforeseen problems, he would reach a trailhead near the highway sometime the next day. It was now well after midnight and time to seek out a place to lay his head. Of course, it would have to be off the beaten path. A place where he could not be seen, or heard or detected by anyone…*searchers or otherwise.*

A short time later, he came out of a heavily forested area into a large open expanse. A creek tumbled noisily down an east-facing slope. The entire mountainside was bathed in moonlight and he could make out a stand of trees about a half mile up. Somewhere at the edge of those trees, he would spend the night. It had taken longer than anticipated to find a suitable location...doesn't it always...and it was far from a perfect. But it was now nearly 2AM, and he was exhausted.

It was almost 8 AM when he awakened. Will stumbled to the creek to fill his water container and then tended to his next priority, a cup of Java and filling his belly with a generous portion of granola.

In less than an hour he hoisted up his backpack and scrambled back down to the trail. The trail was fairly well used, and he would have to be vigilant about meeting other people, but if he had figured out his location correctly, it would lead to to the Granite Creek Trailhead. Here, a dirt road would take him to Rte 2. In the best case scenario, someone at the trailhead would give him a lift to the highway. He would have to take some chances.

Finally arriving at the trailhead, Will struck up a conversation with a young couple who had just arrived from California. They were about to embark upon a ten day adventure into The Bob. Will shared some of the experiences he had had over the last few days...*only the good stuff, of course.*

"Where are you going from here?" the young man asked.

When Will told him, the fellow offered, "Listen, why don't you jump into my pickup. I'll take you to Rte 2, and from there you should be able to hitch a ride to wherever it is you want to go. It's no big deal."

"Are you sure?" Will asked.

"I'm absolutely sure! The young man assured him. "Throw your gear in the back and let's go!"

Will couldn't believe his good fortune. On previous occasions, he had often heard locals make their feelings known. "Don't Californicate Montana!" they would say.

He'd be sure to tell them about this really nice couple from San Francisco.

CHAPTER 27

WILL AND HAL REUNION

A strange tingling sensation came over Will as he stood by the highway, a mixture of fear and anticipation. He had made it this far. Would it be the final dash to freedom, or would he be running straight into the lion's den?

Standing at the side of the road exposed, with his thumb extended would be too risky. Will decided it would be best to remain out of sight as much as possible. A hundred yards down the road was an ideal spot: an outcropping that would allow him a view of approaching traffic, while keeping him hidden. A large spruce for shade was a bonus. He pulled out his binocs.

A "safe" ride would be a foreign make or any hybrid like a Prius. Will couldn't imagine a self-respecting ultra-nationalist driving one of those. A full-sized American brand or a pick-up with a rifle rack and he would remain hidden. Vehicles say a lot about their owners. Stereotyping may have a bad name, but there was something to be said about it!

First came a Subaru Forester with two women. Could be my lucky day he thought to himself. He had a brief flashback to that Lesbian honkytonk back in Georgia. *Is it possible that crazy lark was only a couple of weeks ago?*

Having no sign violated his "Hitchhiking 101" maxims, but perhaps the trauma of the last few days had clouded his judgment. It wouldn't have mattered. Those gals sped by as if he had been wearing an orange prison jumpsuit.

Back to the little hideaway. Traffic was light. Ten minutes went by before the next vehicle approached. The day was also starting to warm up, and with the heat rising off the asphalt, distant vehicles appeared wavy and mirage-like. Still, he could make out a fellow with a straw Stetson behind the wheel of 80s Ford Crown Vic. Most certainly a local. No soliciting a ride from him. Will remained hidden.

It was probably another five minutes before the next vehicle appeared. Will raised his glasses. It was an 80s Ford F-150 pickup with a faded red patina…not good…definitely a local. But as he got a better look, he could make out a driver with a black hat, suspenders and full beard. Recognition kicked in. *That car… could it possibly be?* Was this not his friend, Hal Miller, or had Will just fallen into the all-Hutterites-look-alike-trap?

He grabbed his backpack and rushed to the shoulder. In less than a ten seconds, the vehicle approached at a conservative fifty miles per hour.

Will smiled hopefully…and now he got a better look. Surely that was Hal behind the wheel! But all he got in return was a quick glance, and a rather suspicious one at that. The truck drove by without so much as slowing down. Will's eyes followed hopefully, he kept going. No brake lights. Nothing.

Lowering his thumb in dejection, he stepped off the asphalt back into the shade. What the hell was that all about, he wondered. *Did he not recognize me?*

He hadn't shaved in a week, but still. Will took a last look at the truck which was now a half mile down the road. Then a second look. Were those brake lights he saw? He raised his binocs. Yes, not only brake lights, but the truck had pulled over and was making a u-turn! Will quickly got back to the shoulder. He couldn't help but smile as the vehicle approached.

The pickup slowed down, pulled off to the opposite side of the road. The driver rolled down his window and yelled, "Well, you gonna get in or not?"

"Hal! Damn…darn I mean…it's good to see you! What are you doing up here in Glacier?" Will asked while sprinting across the highway.

"I was up in Alberta for a few days attending the funeral of my cousin, Samuel. Decided to take the scenic route home and get a good look at God's handiwork. It sure is beautiful. I haven't been up in these parts for years!"

Hal moved some packages out of the way for Will to get into the seat. "So how was your little adventure into The Bob?"

Will proceeded to tell him about all the wildlife he saw, with an especially detailed account of the grizzly family. He described the howling of the wolves, and the grouse he killed for dinner. He shared many things, but made no mention of his ordeal at the hands of The Front.

There was a pause in the conversation and then it was Hal who spoke next. "Well, we had a bit of excitement around Choteau. It started maybe a day or so after I dropped you off at The Trail's End. The day before I left for Canada, flyers started appearing all over the place. In fact, a few were dropped off at the colony. I stuck one in the glove compartment. Why don't you take a look.

Will opened the compartment and found a folded piece of paper. He opened it up and could immediately read the word, **"WARNING!"** in bold print. Then in somewhat smaller print, **Do not pick up hitchhikers and be on the lookout for a dangerous man!** Will continued to read.

The following is an advisory for all residents. It was reliably reported that a white, adult male, attempted to molest a fourteen year old boy and honor student yesterday in the vicinity of the high school. Fortunately, the student successfully fought off his attacker and escaped.

The pedophile is described as being of average height and weight, about forty years of age, with short hair and a beard. He speaks with what could be an eastern type accent. He arrived in town recently and several people reported seeing him in a drug induced state or possibly intoxicated. There is a substantial 💰💰💰REWARD💰💰💰 for information leading to his capture.

Many local citizens are presently involved in a search effort. For further information contact Tillman Lee Smith.

In the mean time, it is advised that you do not allow young children to leave home without an adult escort. Please keep your doors and windows locked.

Our peaceful community is once again being menaced by outsiders!

Thank the Lord for the second amendment! Arm yourself in the face of this threat!

Will reflected on those paranoid thoughts he had back in the wilderness. He was not so far off the mark. *Even paranoids are right some of the time!*

Will looked up from the flyer and turned to Hal. "So...what are your thoughts about these things?"

Hal pause for a moment before answering. "Well, I've been around these parts my entire life. I know the insidious nature of rumors and I've seen things like this happen before. Back in the late sixties I think it was, there was that scare around here, a rumor about someone who picked up some hippie hitchhikers and was subsequently killed and cannibalized. It was said the hippies were under the influence of LSD.

Coincidentally, this all took place right after those Charles Manson murders. Of course, there was nothing to the story, but for a long time people were in fear... and terrified of strangers.

Will wanted something more definitive from Hal. "So you don't think there's any truth to this flyer?"

"There's three reasons I don't," Hal explained. "First of all, this piece of paper is nothing official from the state police or county sheriff's department. Second, I personally know some of those fellows hanging up these signs, and we Hutterites know that bunch, Tillman Smith's crowd. We don't get involved in their nonsense. We have our own beliefs.

You know, those people claim to be God-fearing, patriotic Christian Americans, but I tell you, they have a strange way of interpreting the teachings of Christ! As for their patriotism, based on our history, Hutterites are rightfully skeptical of their brand of patriotism!

Will, you teach history, so I'll ask you a question. Are you familiar with the quote, 'Patriotism is the last refuge of the scoundrel'? And for two extra points on your test, who said it and when?" he chuckled.

Will's reply came quickly. "It was back in England, 1775 I believe, by Samuel Johnson... actually one of my favorite quotes."

"You're good, Mr. Kraft. Your students are lucky to have you as a teacher!"

"Thanks, Hal...maybe you can share that with my superintendent of schools back home."

"Why do you need me for that?"

"Never mind," said Will, "just rambling. By the way, Hal, what's the third reason. You said there were three reasons you put no stock in these posters."

"Did I say three?"

"You did, but don't worry. It's not important."

"But I did say three, didn't I? So there has to be a third. When I come up with it, I'll be sure to tell you!" Hal laughed at his last remark. "But think about it. If I thought there was any credence to those signs, would I have picked you up?"

"I guess not," Will acknowledged. *But why did Hal first pass me by before he stopped and turned around? Why was he hesitant at first? Surely he recognized me. So maybe he was just a bit dubious about this stranger from New York, that he might not be the person he seemed to be.* Will then thought that perhaps it was best to put aside these doubts. He would simply place his trust in Hal and tell him what needs to be told.

"Hal," Will began with a deep breath, "I'm going to tell you something. I'm going out on a limb here, but I'm hoping you can help me." After a pause, he continued. "Hal, I did have a run-in with some local fellows who are undoubtedly the ones behind those signs. I have no idea who they were, or for that matter what they looked like, with maybe the exception of one of them, a kind of low IQ guy named 'Donny'".

"Donny? Hal questioned. "Donny Jackson? About six foot tall, skinny…maybe hundred and fifty pounds, long, straggly, blondish hair…?"

"Never got his last name, but you describe him perfectly."

"Funny thing is, I just saw Donny a few days ago fueling up at the gas station. His pickup was loaded, and he was hauling an open trailer loaded with loads of personal stuff, and a mattress and some furniture. It wasn't packed very well, even for Donny. I asked Donny, where you off to? He said off to California. I asked why California. He said it's where there's more opportunity. I assumed he meant work. Now who's going to hire a fellow like Donny I asked myself. I know him real well since he was a kid. He was certainly acting strange, or scared maybe."

Hal pulled into a gas station with a small café. He parked his pickup in the shade of an old tree toward the back of the parking area. Then he reached behind the seat and came up with a black Hutterite hat. "Wait here," Hal instructed, "and put this hat over your face. Pretend you're sleeping. I'll be back in a couple of minutes with coffee and a slice of huckleberry pie. Then you can tell me the rest of your story. How do you like your coffee?"

"Dark, one sugar."

Will pulled the hat over his face and slid down into the seat. He leaned his head against the side window. A minute later, Hal returned with two coffees and two slices of pie.

"You're probably hungry, Will," said Hal compassionately, "but let's drive a little ways to a place that's more private. Then you can tell me more."

A few miles later, Hal pulled off into an unpaved ranch road, and before long they were parked in the shade of a pair of massive cottonwoods beside a gravelly creek."

"Not too many folks come down here," cautioned Hal, "but if someone does, same thing as I told you before. Pull that hat down over your face and pretend you're sleeping." There was a momentary pause. "Now tell me what happened."

Will continued the story of his encounter with The Front and how he was kidnapped as part of a hare-brained scheme to hold him for a ransom that his "wealthy Jewish family" would surely pay. Then he told Hal the part about how they discovered he wasn't Jewish, and the uproar that ensued, and how they began to squabble amongst themselves, giving him the opportunity to escape.

Hal listened with amazement and not a small amount of incredulity. Several times he had to ask Will to back up and explain certain parts.

All along, Will was wondering if Hal could possibly believe such a preposterous story. *Perhaps it had been a mistake to confide in him, after all.*

"So what now?" wondered Hal aloud.

"Well somehow I need to get back to Missoula. For one thing, I have a suitcase waiting for me at the hotel with identification and some money. Did I mention that those bas...uh, people, took my wallet? In Missoula there's a federal building where I hope to speak to the right folks in the FBI, and..."

"I can help you with that, Will. But first… and I hope you don't take this the wrong way…you, my friend, are in serious need of a shower!"

"I was hoping It wasn't that noticeable…"

"You can 'hope' all you want, Will. We need to take a quick detour back to the colony. You can take your shower and get your clothes presentable. Then we'll get you back to Missoula."

"By the way," interjected Will, "this is some fine huckleberry pie!"

"It better be good!" Hal puffed his chest. "My wife and daughters bake it back at the colony. The locals love it."

"I'll bet it has no artificial stuff in it and no preservatives."

"Preservatives? Don't need no preservatives… it never sits around long enough!"

An uncomfortable silence followed which was broken when Hal finally spoke again. "I just remembered reason three."

"What are you talking about…'reason three'?" Will asked.

"A while back, I told you there were three reasons I didn't believe there was any truth to those warning posters. I gave you two, but said the third reason had escaped me, but now I just remembered it"

Hal then took a deep breath. "I believe that God has given me certain abilities, and among them is the ability to look into a person's …soul. To be able to look into that soul and judge a person's fundamental character. Over the years, I've never been wrong in that regard. That's why many of my people back in the colony come to me for advice. Not that I have any sort of official capacity in those matters, it's just that it seems to have worked out that way.

When we first met over a week ago, back when I picked you up hitchhiking, I could tell that you were a person of upright character. I also suspected when I read those flyers being handed out, that there was a good chance that it was *you* they were referring to. Now I don't know what your personal spiritual beliefs are, and I know they're certainly not the same as mine, but that makes no difference. It comes down to this: I believe your story, and because I believe it, I'm going to do what I can to help you!"

"Now let's get back to the colony," Miller said abruptly. "My kids and the wife will be glad to see you!"

They got back into the cab, Hal started the engine, and before long they were back on the highway. The colony was not far, and along the way, Hal and Will continued to discuss a plan of action. The road was empty. In the past fifteen minutes, they saw only one other vehicle, pretty much the norm for this stretch of pavement.

Then they saw a second vehicle parked facing them on the other side of the highway, a rather unusual one: a 1984 Mercedes Gelandeswagen, known to afficianadoes as the G-Wagen. This particular one was impressively tricked out with special lights, wheels and a "snorkel". It was clearly intended for serious off-road use, but like so many rigs with that kind of money invested in them, it probably never left paved highways.

"Wow," commented Will, scoping out the G-Wagen, "that guy must be a celebrity or someone from California. You don't see too many of those around here!"

As they passed the vehicle, Hal continued to watch the side view mirror. He knew that the big Mercedes belonged to Tillman Smith. That had him worried. Then Hal saw its brake lights flash, and the back-up lights flicker. In an instant the G-Wagen had made a u-turn.

"Will," Hal announced, "I know that rig! It's not from California, and we are officially in the midst of a bad situation! Cinch up your seat belt and hang on!"

Hal stomped on the gas pedal and the big V-8 awakened with a roar. In less than ten seconds the speedometer reached the century mark. The truck shifted into high gear, and continued its climb into uncharted territory.

"I had no idea this old girl had it in her!" Hal was heard to yell above the engine's roar. Glancing quickly into the rear- view mirror, he saw nothing. "We lost 'em!"

His exultation was a bit premature. In a matter of seconds, the Gelandeswagen was back in the rear view mirrors, gaining rapidly. Hal then put the truck up high into the next curve, and to Will's astonishment, hit the brakes while cutting the steering wheel sharply to the left. The big truck drifted sideways into a perfect 90 degree turn, wheels churning and spinning, then rattled across a set of cattle grates onto an unpaved ranch road.

A Hutterite channeling Dale Earnhardt?

"How'd you learn to drive like that, Hal?" yelled Will above the roar.

"Watching a lot of car chase movies… Steve McQueen driving that 'Bullitt' Mustang. 'The French Connection'… 'Smokey and the Bandit'… the first one where he flies across the collapsed bridge in his TransAm…"

"But they used professional stunt drivers," Will protested. "By the way, I think we may have lost them…" Those words barely left his mouth when he glanced back into the side view mirror and caught a pair of rapidly approaching, dust-piercing halogens.

"Now what, Hal?" Will shouted, now clearly terrified.

"Plan B!" Hal yelled loudly.

"Plan B?" screamed Will even louder.

"B…as in BRIDGE!" Hal shouted. "Hang on, Will!!!"

Once again, Hal hit the brakes and slid into another side road in another laws-of-physics- defying turn. Off to his right, Will could make out a shiny new Highway Department sign announcing:

DANGER! BRIDGE OUT AHEAD- ROAD CLOSED!

"Hal…Hal.. did you see?…"

"I know…I know," Hal assured Will. "I've got this one!"

The speedometer reached seventy, feeling more like a hundred on the unpaved road. At eighty, Hal drove through a wooden barricade, shattering it into toothpicks. Then came a slight rise and a thirty foot void where a bridge once stood. It had been constructed by the CCC back during the Great Depression. Ten years ago, highway engineers deemed it unsafe and shortly after, it was demolished and never replaced. The only evidence that a bridge ever stood here was the pair of stone and concrete pillars that once supported the span…and of course, the **DANGER!** Sign.

In the rapidly flowing river below, cutthroat trout were feasting on a hatch of caddis flies. They scattered for safety when an unexpected shadow was cast upon them. Further downstream, a family of otters with three pups had been frolicking along the bank when they heard a roar and felt a tremble. They looked up in alarm at the sight of a two ton projectile hurtling across their secluded playground.

As for Will, he had no time to engage in academic exercises such as employing the formula for trajectory ($y = h + x * \tan(a) - g * x2 / 2* Vo2 * \cos2 (a)$) to determine the outcome of the launch (although the following year he would consult with a physics teacher colleague on the matter).

Right now, he was frozen in terror, one hand with a death grip on the door handle and the other braced against the dash with a force that would leave a permanent imprint.

As for Hal, there appeared on his face a beatific smile, and a barely perceptible movement of the lips. Any vocalizations were drowned out by the roar of the engine and the larynx-shattering scream of Will sitting in—what is it called—the "suicide-seat"?

In later years, Hal, always a masterful story-teller, would insist that he was singing the words from that popular song of the sixties, "Michael", by the Highwaymen.

The river is deep and the river is wide,
Hallelujah
Milk and honey on the other side
Hallelujah

That became Hal's version of the events that unfolded, that to this day he will enthusiastically share with anyone who cares to listen.

Back to the actual event. The F-150, subject to the inescapable laws of physics (as determined by the trajectory formula…), did eventually touch down, about ten feet beyond the far bank (a total distance of forty six feet, eight inches for the detail obsessed) in a spring twisting- shock absorber mangling- drive shaft bending- muffler destroying not to mention bone rattling- jaw crunching- vertebrae compressing- gluteal squishing- sphincter rending… landing. Miraculously, the twenty year old truck, though forever compromised, remained capable of forward motion.

As the pickup limped onward. Hal and Will took a moment to look behind them. They watched as the G-Wagon came to a sliding halt inches before the river's edge. Doors flew open, and occupants jumped out, shouting and waving their arms.

With its exhaust system now barely hanging from the chassis, Hal's pickup emitted a terrible roar. Still, they were able to limp away from their pursuers. Hal looked down at the oil pressure and temperature gauges, and cautiously gave the vehicle a clean bill-of-health.

A mile or so down the road they stopped to conduct a more thorough check underneath the truck and test their own body parts as well! Hal had a flamboyant fat lip from hitting the steering wheel. Will's right knee would likely require the services of an orthopedist. The truck's engine was loud, but the crankcase was miraculously intact.

But what was that new noise? *Thwap- thwap- thwap- thwap...*

As Hal and Will watched in astonishment, two FBI Bell 407 helicopters descended upon the road, one behind, and one in front of them. Within seconds, eight agents were disgorged with enough weaponry to overthrow a third-world government.

CHAPTER 28

COMING BACK DOWN TO EARTH

Hal and Will found themselves strapped into helicopter seats, a novel experience for both of them. While polite enough, the FBI agents asked them to remain quiet until they arrived at their destination, a flight of about twenty minutes. The agents assured them that they were in safe hands.

Hal stared down at the pastureland, farms and forests below. Though the terrain was familiar to him, he had never before seen it from above. In fact, he had never been in any aircraft before, and found himself enjoying the experience.

The helicopter was soon hovering over a make-shift landing pad on a parcel of land that Hal recognized. On the property, however, stood an unfamiliar cluster of trailers the FBI had set up, their command post.

Several days earlier, under cover of darkness, a hundred- person FBI team had descended upon the area. They had commenced a pre-dawn raid on about twenty residences that had been previously identified as homes of Front members. Simultaneously with the home raids, the FBI set up their own little village of trailers that would serve as both interrogation rooms and holding pens.

Highly skilled teams of three to four agents entered each of the homes, with search warrants. One of those homes belonged to the Jackson family.

Donny's father was still in bed when the agents burst in. His first groggy words were, "I suppose this might have something to do with Tillman Smith."

Not a shot was fired in the operation. The sweep resulted in the arrest of 28 individuals and the confiscation of a total of 862 weapons, about 600 of which were found in one hay barn. They were stored with the intent of being distributed to other right -wing militias throughout northern Montana and Idaho.

In addition to weaponry, an enormous cache of hate literature was discovered. The pamphlets and posters targeted Jews, Muslims, Hispanics, homosexuals, and *Coastal Elites.*

The operation was a tactical success. Twentyeight of the original thirty targeted individuals were now in custody. Two men who eluded capture were Donny Jackson and Pete Anderson.

At the time of the raid, Jackson was already on the road somewhere between Montana and California hauling an overloaded trailer filled with personal possessions. He knew that Tillman Smith was angry with him, and he had heard the stories of what happens to those who crossed him. Though he had been in a hurry to get out of Montana, he had taken the time to put together a "to-do-list" for when he finally got to California. The handwritten list was clipped to the dashboard. At the top of the list was *"Look up Plastic Surgins ".*

A day later he was stopped at the California Agricultural Inspection Station on Interstate 40. Such stations are charged with the function of preventing invasive species of plants and animals from entering the Golden State.

Donny's trailer contained a rather gross and soiled mattress and other suspicious looking cargo, and to the inspector at least, Donny himself looked like one of those Dust-Bowl Okies he had recently seen while watching "The Grapes of Wrath" on the Turner Classic Movie network.

The inspector decided to not wave him on. He needed to ask a few questions.

"Sir, where are you from?"

"Montana…"

"…are you transporting fruits or vegetables in your vehicle or trailer… or any animals"?

Maybe it was the heat of the Nevada desert that Donny was forced to endure in his old un-air conditioned Chevy pickup. The broken radio didn't help matters, either. Any number of things may have affected his response. Then again, maybe it was just Donny being Donny. But he just couldn't get himself to simply answer, "No sir!"

It was understandable. After all, he had been driving the featureless highways for hours and thirsted for human interaction… of any kind. What he said to the man in uniform was, "Sir, I do admit to transporting a half-eaten container of guacamole…does that count"?

The inspector was not amused.

So Donny tried harder. "But if you're wondering if I'm harboring a ferret or marmot like the one those Krauts threw into the Dude's bathtub, I swear I do not have any such contraband…Sir!"

Having never seen that movie, "The Big Lebowski", the ferret reference was completely lost on the inspector. He gave Donny a blank, but increasingly irritated look.

At this point, anybody else would have left well enough alone, but feeling somewhat miffed at the apparent absence of any sense of humor on the part of the official, Donny chose to continue. "By the way, thousands of you people come up to visit our beautiful state of Montana every year just to see what our country looked like before it got so fucked-up, just sayin'. Do we stop you folks at our border to ask if you're carrying any California products like salt-water taffy or child pornography? You have a hell of a nerve…"

"**Sir!** Please pull your vehicle over to the area on the right," demanded the inspector, pointing to an area of pavement with a sign reading 'ENHANCED INSPECTION ZONE'. **Immediately!"**

It was too late for a retraction or any sort, or an apology from Donny. An alarm had already been sounded, and in seconds, two ChiPs (California Highway Patrol) vehicles screeched into position, effectively boxing in Donny's pickup. Before you could say "Arnold Alois Schwarzenegger", four highway patrolmen wearing scowls and Ray-Bans had their Tazers drawn. A phone call to Montana confirmed that Jackson was indeed, a dangerous fugitive from justice. He was taken into custody.

At the time of the FBI raid on Choteau, Pete Anderson, aka Pete Andrews, the inebriate from Cour d'Alene, who had enthralled members of The Front with the notion that terrorism in the service of patriotism was "righteous activism", yes, that Pete, was in a sleazy motel somewhere in the Idaho panhandle. He was sleeping off a not- insignificant hangover with a skanky barmaid he had fallen in love with the previous night at the bewitching hour of 3 AM. It was now 8am. He did manage to open one eye, but became so alarmed at the sight next to him, that he willed himself back into a coma.

Anyway, Pete had been watching the newscast on a local TV station and that's how he learned about the raid. Already in Idaho, he promptly sought refuge in a small abandoned homesteaders cabin up in the Bitterroots. There, he would live off the local flora and fauna, leaving only once a month to go into town to replenish his liquor supply. He managed to elude capture for another five years until his liver gave out. Folks were surprised to learn that he was only 43 years old. Most guessed him to be closer to seventy.

You surely recall Aaron Barber, the muscular, bad -ass, quintessential Aryan who took part in the interrogation of Will Kraft at the headquarters of The Front. The same Aaron Barber who had killed a Mexican drug gang member with his bare hands and had spent eight years in Huntsville. He too had been taken into "custody", but it was all for show. It turns out that his real name was Mathias Keller.

Keller was raised in West Bend, Wisconsin where his mother and father both taught at the local high school. He, along with his other two brothers had stood out both academically and athletically in high school. Matthias wound up attending the University of Wisconsin on a full-ride. As a college senior, he placed third in the 174 lb weight class in the NCAA Division I Wrestling Tournament. After graduating magna cum laude, he was recruited by the FBI.

Keller's performance as a special agent was exemplary. He soon moved on to become an intelligence agent specializing in domestic terrorism. An adrenalin junkie, he requested undercover work. Shortly after, he was assigned to investigate the operations of right-wing extremists. The Front was a perfect organization to infiltrate.

Agent Keller had worked undercover, investigating The Front for six months. During that time he was wired and in constant danger of being discovered. Although the group was detestable, he never felt he had gathered sufficient information for serious indictments. The kidnapping of Will Kraft took Keller by complete surprise. He was convinced that he had misjudged the group and should have acted sooner. No one was more relieved when Will managed to escape.

The very same evening of the kidnapping, Keller had contacted the FBI Field Office in Salt Lake City and they pulled the trigger on "Operation Big Sky" (OBS). Within two days, the roundup was essentially completed.

As far as the car chase goes, it was brought about by a misunderstanding and perhaps an error in judgement on the part of Agent Keller. He and three other agents had just confiscated Tillman Smith's G-Wagen and were in the process of delivering it to the FBI Command Post, when they pulled over to the side of the highway to take a phone call from headquarters.

Then Gelandeswagen was one of many toys that Smith had amassed while leader of The Front. Apparently, not all the money donated by sympathizers went toward The Front's "educational programs". Much of it was co-mingled with Smith's personal assets, which he used to purchase the $100K Mercedes and much of the expensive art-work in The Front's headquarters.

The agents happened to be sitting in that car alongside the highway just as Hal Miller and Will came driving by. Keller spotted Will in the passenger seat and shouted, "There goes our guy!" And the race was on.

Hal, of course, immediately recognized the vehicle, but not yet knowing anything about the FBI operation, naturally assumed that he was being pursued by Tillman Smith. Which is why he put the pedal-to-the-metal. Hal's actions took Keller by complete surprise. After all, Miller was a Hutterite. Keller assumed it would be as easy as displaying their badges, and the pickup would pull over, end of story.

Later in custody, when Hal explained his actions, the FBI saw no reason to not believe him. He had been up in Canada attending a funeral. How could he have known anything about "Operation Big Sky" or the fact that Smith's vehicle had been commandeered by the FBI? Hal's decision to try and outrun the pursuing vehicle made sense.

The Agents offered to have one of their medics treat Hal's fat lip, but Hal declined. He was understandably anxious to return to the colony.

Since his pickup was deemed undrivable, an agent drove him back in a civilian vehicle so as not to cause an uproar. The FBI asked him to remain in touch in case they had to ask him further questions.

"Where would I go?" was all Hal said in reply.

Will learned much of this while being interviewed by Special Agents Betsy Olsen and Hank Stokowski. While Will had a million questions, the agents shared only as much detail as they thought was necessary. Many of his questions were met with, "We're not at liberty to provide such information at the moment due to the ongoing investigation."

One of the questions the agents did answer was whether or not Will's family was in harm's way. While the agents had no reason to believe that the family was in danger, they assured him that his wife and children were being protected. Will had little choice but to believe them.

Will stayed with the OBS team for a few more days. He was asked to give a statement about his entire ordeal: his arrival in Choteau, the night at the Jackelope, the kidnapping, his captivity and subsequent escape, the time spent in the Bob and his reuniting with Hal Miller. He was then given permission to return home.

The FBI took care of airline reservations and got him on a flight to New York. An agent drove him to Missoula, where Will picked up his suitcase at the hotel. The young concierge, Wyatt was on duty at the front desk. Recognizing Will, Wyatt excitedly asked about his backpacking adventure.

"Incredibly relaxing," replied Will, "I only wish there had been more wild life."

CHAPTER 29

THE FLYING HOOT

Following the high-speed chase, some interesting and unforeseen developments took place in Hal Miller's life. As one can imagine, it was hard to keep a secret in a small Montana town. Folks in the community quickly learned about the FBI roundup, and the fact that one of their own, Hal Miller the Hutterite, played a role in the drama that unfolded. Despite being counseled to not say a word, Hal, always a gifted storyteller, could not just sit quietly on one of the best stories ever.

It didn't take long for the chase story and Hal's incredible leap over the river to become legend. The entire episode, including color photos of Hal and his F-150 pickup as well as the old bridge site where the leap took place, appeared in the Sunday magazine section of the Great Falls Tribune. TV stations throughout the Upper Midwest and Rocky Mountain states also covered the story.

Hal actually received a request from David Letterman to appear on The Late Show, a request he respectfully declined, explaining that he didn't think he could manage to stay up that late. Letterman, himself, incidentally, reported that there was no truth to the story going around that his decision to retire to the Choteau area was influenced by Miller's exploits. "Hell, I retired to a ranch out here to get away from drama," said Letterman in a recent interview, "there's far too much excitement going on in Hal Miller's life for me!"

Hal's Ford pickup was purchased pretty much sight unseen by an enterprising Ford dealer and flat-bedded to his dealership in Great Falls. It's now on permanent display in front of the showroom. There's a historical marker with detailed information about the incident, including an artist's rendering of the 46' 8" "leap", the time of the "flight" and technical data about the 1984 Ford F-150. Of course, there's also a great deal of biographical information about the man who piloted the pickup, better known these days as "The Flying Hoot".

Expect a crowd if you plan to visit. With the passage of time, the leap across the river has achieved Evel Knievel type fame. Isn't that just human nature? Despite concerns on the part of colony elders, "The Flying Hoot" display has become a popular destination for Hutterite school groups. It attracts others as well, like Ford F-150 enthusiasts, Japanese tour groups and of course, German tourists, who love that off-beat stuff.

According to the Great Fall's Visitors Bureau, the number of tourists going to see that quirky display now rivals the Charley Russell Museum. Visitors are advised to arrive early.

CHAPTER 30

A PILE OF MAIL

———⟨∿⟩———

A few weeks after returning to Long Island, Will received two letters. One from Martin and Iris Wetzel, Stuttgart, Germany, and the other from Henry Hawksbill, "Hawk".

He first opened the one from his German friends.

Liebe Will,

We hope that this letter finds you in good health and refreshed by your *Wanderung* in the Montana wilderness. After all, is that not why we go on holiday?

We want to again tell you how much we enjoyed our time together at the Little Big Horn Battle Site. The story of how you buried the items from the battle for your Native-American friend "Hawk" is something we have shared with many of our friends here in Germany. Ourfellow Indian *Hobbyists* were not believing us.. They are thinking perhaps that we are telling them a "Tall Tale", trying to be like Baron von Munchhausen.

May we ask, did you ever made contact with "Hawk"? and what was his response? You told us that by burying the *Artefakte?* you hoped to restore *Ruhe (peace?)* to his trouble soul. If you contact Hawk, did he tell you anything that helped you know your efforts were successful? Of course, since Iris and I played a small role in your project, perhaps we would be permitted to take some pride in its success?

After we left you, the rest of our journey through the Dakotas, Wyoming and Montana was quite enjoyable. I must say, American drivers do frighten us however. Is it really OK to pass on the right on your *Autobahns*? We also hoped to see more Indians on horses and not in their big pickup trucks, but perhaps we are more than a hundred years late for this, yes?

We did attend several festivals and powwows and were, how do Americans say, dazzled by the dancing and colorful costumes. The Indian Relays at the Crow Fair were *ausgezeichnet*. We especially enjoyed the powwow at Heart Butte. It was *sehr authentisch*.

I must confess that when we visited the Bear Paw Battlefield and read Chief Joseph's Surrender Speech (*From Where the sun now stands I will fight no more forever*) we both cried. So *traurig(sad?)*!

You might enjoy this little story. At Heart Butte, we were able to find an old man who was willing to have a conversation with us in the Lakota language. He smiled the entire time. Iris and I think it is either that our language skills are not so good, or perhaps he was so surprised to hear his language coming from the mouths of two German people. I can also imagine that hearing Lakota spoken with a German accent is just very funny.

Please keep in touch and hopefully you will visit us in Germany some day. You spoke of your interest in European History. I don't think we are able to help you experience anything quite so exciting as what we did at Little Big Horn, but we can try!

Ihre Freunden,
Iris and Martin Wetzel

Sitting back, smiling about the contact with his new German friends, Will remembered he had another letter to read. He opened Hawk's letter.

Dear Will,

Just writing to ask how the rest of your travels went and how was your time in the Bob Marshall Wilderness. I hate to be a pain, but did you ever get a chance to bury those items at the Little Big Horn Battle Site? After making the request, I started to have second thoughts. I realized I may have been a bit selfish, and that you might be getting yourself into trouble on my account. So if you were unable to do this, I understand. Just please send those items back to me, if you would.

It may not even be necessary for those items to be placed back into the soil at Little Big Horn anyway. It's been over a month now, and quite honestly, a few days after we met, I stopped having that recurring dream. To be more accurate, a new dream has taken its place. In this new dream, the white man and I finally meet and travel together as brothers into the beautiful valley I spoke of. We learn to share it's abundance. I know this must sound a bit far-fetched, but that's just the way dreams are!

If you wouldn't mind, get back to me one way or the other.

Your *Ne'se'ne,*

Henry "Hawk" Hawksbill

PS I hope my boy, Pete, took good care of you back at the motel!

Will responded first to the German couple. He enclosed a copy of Hawk's letter for them to read. Next he composed a reply to Hawk. In that letter, he shared the entire improbable adventure of burying the artifacts with the assistance of two Indian-loving German tourists. He never even hinted at the possibility that the interment of those artifacts had anything to do with the change in Hawk's dream world. It would be better if he left Hawk to arrive at that conclusion on his own.

CHAPTER 31

LOOSE ENDS

---◦ᡕ᠊◦---

Upon his return home, Will had met with the lawyer assigned to his case by the teacher's union. Will still wasn't so sure about her competence. She was young and inexperienced and had graduated near the bottom of her class at Baruch Law School in Manhattan: that was the bad news. The good news? She was full of enthusiasm and anxious to make a name for herself. After a thorough review of the circumstances of Will's firing, she confidently declared, "I think I'm going to win my first case here!" Not exactly what a client wants to hear from a lawyer.

As it turned out, it wasn't irrational exuberance. The circumstances surrounding Will's dismissal were so blatantly illegal, that he was reinstated after a hearing lasting only fifteen minutes. The hearing officer was so angered over the school district "...wasting my valuable time with its frivolous and petty actions..." that he not only ruled in Will's favor, but issued a stern warning to the entire administration from the superintendent down to the principal. The district was placed on probation, with all future personnel decisions subject to review by the State Education Department.

Will was back in his classroom on opening day of the new school year. Deciding it would be best to be proactive regarding the pledge, he read to his class a summary of one the many Supreme Court decisions pertaining to the recital of the pledge in schools. The decisions were pretty much all in agreement that students are not required to recite or stand during the Pledge of Allegiance.

He also expressed his gratitude for "the good fortune of living in a free country whose constitution grants citizens the kinds of civil liberties that the United States of America does."

When the pledge came over the P.A. system, Will promptly stood up. Looking around, he was relieved to see all of his students standing as well. *This will be a good year* he thought to himself. His recitation was emphatic and forceful, if not theatrical, so it was obvious to his students when he omitted the "under God" portion. He did take his civil liberties seriously!

As far as the marriage, nothing changed. After learning all about Will's Montana saga, Katie did express second thoughts about the divorce, and suggested marriage counseling.

During his time hitchhiking across the land, and then alone with his thoughts in The Bob, Will had been able to make a sober assessment of the last few years of his marriage. He understood that the relationship had truly reached a point of no return. Quite honestly, the growing happiness between himself and Annie had something to do with his decision as well. Will declined to enter counseling.

With the guidance of a professional mediator, the marriage was officially terminated six months to the day after he was served with papers. He would share custody of the children with Kate. Will found himself a modest but very cool apartment in an old stable that was formerly part of an estate on Long Island's North Shore... the "Gold Coast".

Sometime in November, Will received a letter from, of all people, Mathias Keller aka Aaron Barber. In his correspondence, Keller apologized for not being able to share any of the details of the case he was helping to prepare in Federal Court: *The United States Government vs The Front.* Mathias simply wanted to take a moment to thank Will for the courage and resourcefulness he displayed during his ordeal.

Mathias had also written to inform Will that he would be flown to Salt Lake City on at least two occasions to serve as a witness for the prosecution. For his protection, he would not actually take the witness stand. Using a device to change his voice, he would be questioned by both defense lawyers and federal prosecutors as well.

At the trial's conclusion, only five defendants would be found guilty of very serious felonies that included kidnapping, assault, hate crimes, denial of civil rights along with a host of federal gun law offenses. The person receiving the lengthiest sentence was not surprisingly, Donny Jackson: twenty five years.

Tillman Smith, The Front's charismatic leader, was able to secure the services of a talented West Coast law firm, Moskowitz, Goldstein and Cohen (Smith referred to them as his "Hebrew Dream Team"). They were able to secure a 'not guilty' verdict for some of the more serious felony charges. The gun trafficking charge, however, was pretty clear cut. All in all, it was unlikely that Smith's actual jail time would amount to more than seven and a half years. It's complicated.

CHAPTER 32

NOUVEAU RICHE

———∿———

Although somewhat oblique to everything that took place, it would be unfair to not share some interesting developments regarding Will's dad, Ernie. You recall that when Will visited his folks in Ponce deLeon Estates, he discovered that his dad had become afflicted with a strange late-in-life foot/shoe fetish. To describe it as a perversion would be a stretch. Hell, a lot more kinkier things go on in senior citizen communities...folks have no idea!

The way Ernie Kraft tells it, he and his buddy, Pete Magee were enjoying a cold beer after tennis one afternoon, when the subject of snakes came up. It had been a story on the evening news. Specifically, the alarm over the growing number of exotic pythons slithering all over the Everglades and the ecological devastation they were wreaking.

Then came an brilliant idea: What if these beautifully exotic snake skins could be used in the manufacture of ladies shoes? Surely not a new idea, but the genius part had to do with the marketing scheme. The shoes would be promoted as a solution to the snake problem!

Ernie went on to describe how, in a matter of a few months, they were able to sell the idea to the renowned Italian women's shoe designer, Gino Calzolaio. Together, they formed a partnership, creating a new company that manufactured exquisite high-heeled shoes made from the skins of Burmese pythons, anacondas and other cold-blooded killers, all harvested in the Everglades.

The product went by the name "Serpentino Stilettos". They would be sold in exclusive department stores and boutiques in Miami, Boca Raton, Naples and Sarasota. In advertisements, it was claimed that 50% of the profits would be donated toward restoration of the Everglades ecosystem (Since the killing of these invasive snakes was a necessary part of the supply chain for the raw material, and somebody had to pay for the skins, the claim was legitimate if not a bit misleading).

The marketing firm created ads featuring lovely women's legs with pronounced calf muscles, alongside Disney-like images of fawns and baby bunnies. A bold "Save the Everglades!" sticker was affixed to each shoe box. The message was clear: by purchasing Serpentinos, thousands of innocent and adorable creatures would be spared from the rapacious reptiles.

It was astonishing how quickly the product caught on. Retailers had a hard time keeping up with inventory. Soon every Floridian woman of means owned at least one pair of Serpentinos. At every social event and fund-raiser, at every celebrity wedding and bar mitzvah, women wanted to be seen in the incredibly expensive snake skin footwear.

Riding boots were added to the line and were all the rage at the Palm Beach International Equestrian Center. The young lady who placed first at the Miss Universe of Miami Beauty Pageant? She sported Serpentinos. After the initial frenzy, there was a slight decline in sales. The decision was made to jack the price up fifty percent. Once again, shoes began flying off the shelves!

As with any business, the remarkable success of Serpentinos did not occur without incident.

There was that lawsuit filed by Florida Friends of Reptiles. The organization claimed discrimination against the class *Reptilia,* and that the butchering of the snakes was "wanton and cruel". The lawyer representing Serpentinos appeared in court with videos documenting that their suppliers (good -ol'- boy crackers dressed more professionally for the films) performed the deeds humanely. Representatives from the Florida Audubon Society were also brought on board to defend the "euthanizing" of the enormous, invasive serpents. It's no great secret that when it comes to arousing sympathy, feathers will trump scales every time, no offense to the herpetology community which surely includes some fine people. The case against Serpentinos never stood a chance!

Then came the incident that took place in Mizner Park, the luxury shopping mall in beautiful downtown Boca Raton. One day, among the crowd of well dressed shoppers entering the mall, there appeared a bearded (...and barefooted) young man donning a tattered robe and carrying a long wooden staff.

Of course, the security guards spotted him immediately. One suggested that he was an actor from that Holy Land Experience theme park that had recently opened in Orlando, maybe auditioning for a role. Another conjectured that he was a hippy that had strayed into the wrong decade. The guards agreed to follow him, but at a cautious distance.

Anyway, the robed man continued to stroll into the mall. He eventually positioned himself in front of the boutique carrying Serpentino Stilettos and proceeded to deliver a sermon entitled, "Do You Have a Hole in your Sole" (...or was it S-O-U-L?)

The young manager of the store had landed his position on the strength of a resume' that hinted at the marketing classes he had been enrolled in at a community college in south Florida. Although he had flunked out after the first semester, one thing he did take away from his experience was the axiom one of his professors often quoted, "there's no such thing as 'bad' publicity." With this in mind, the manager requested that security adopt a *laissez-faire* approach to the eccentric young man.

So the sermons were allowed to continue, and in fact they did, five times a day for three straight days, attracting curious and sizable crowds. The local news channel even sent a reporter and camera crew to cover the event. But this was Boca, and the self-described prophet's admonitions against materialism and consumerism went unheeded. In fact, Serpentino sales increased by fifty percent over that three- day period and continued upward thereafter.

Will's parents became rich overnight. "Nouveau riche" is what we are," proclaimed Will's dad. "Heck, a year ago, I didn't even know what that word meant!"

Will suggested to his dad that he now had enough money to sell the double-wide in Ponce deLeon Estates and perhaps buy a nice house in Sarasota or down in Naples. His dad made some crack about not wanting to be like the "Beverly Hillbillies." But Ernie Kraft was generous enough with his recently acquired wealth to replace Will's old Astro Van with a new car. Of course, it meant that Will could no longer win that faculty pool.

CHAPTER 33

FIFTEEN MINUTES OF FAME

―――∿――――

Andy Warhol once predicted a future in which each person would be world famous for fifteen minutes. Of course, that quote subsequently took on a life of its own, but how could Will have known that he personally would actually live out such an eventuality?

He had just gotten back into the swing of the new school year. A few days before Thanksgiving, a letter arrived from of all people, Tommy Lee "Mudpuppy" Clarke. It took a few seconds for the name to register. It then came back to him. It was the fellow that headed that band down in Georgia, "The Mysterious Mudpuppies". He had almost forgotten about that crazy night.

Will opened the letter and read:

To the 'Dancin' Fool, Will Kraft,

I don't give a shit what Neil Young says, a "Southern Man" is an honest man, and the band and me decided that you're entitled to a share of the royalties. Just sign the enclosed contract. (You do know, I hope, that your little "Lesbian Girl" ditty is starting to get a bit of attention in the music world?) I trust that 20% is enough. We'll instruct the record company to send future checks up to you on "Lawn Guyland". Is this satisfactory? Enclosed you'll find your first check for $253.22.

BTW you might be interested in the enclosed article I cut out of a music trade publication.

Rock on!

Tommy Lee "Mudpuppy" Clarke

Will unfolded the article written by a prominent music critic that Clarke had inserted into the envelope. He read the part Hi-Lited in yellow. "Only the heart strings of the most seriously jaded country music listener will not be twanged by the lyrics of 'Lesbian Girl', a trailblazing ballad of unrequited love and fragile male ego..."

I'll be damned, thought Will, *I've become a trailblazer!*

And the rest is history, as they say. Those Mudpuppy boys took Will's lyrics, tweaked them a bit, set them to a country waltz. Later that year, "I Fell in Love with a Lesbian Girl" would rise to number six on the Alternative Country Music chart. If there had been a *Lesbian Alternative Country* category, the song would have probably won a Grammy. The *Mudpuppies* were decent enough to allow Will to sign a contract which made his percentage of the royalties official. He was soon amazed at how much a few pennies a play would add up.

Prior to recording this breakthrough song, the *Mudpuppies* were kind of a local band playing in bars and roadhouses in the Southeast. With that one new song, their notoriety spread. They began doing gigs as far north as Boston at venues with real cachet like the Beacon Theater in *The Big Apple*. They even hired a manager, an extremely capable young lady, to take care of bookings and the business end. Will, of course, was delighted in their new-found success, and allowed himself to take a small amount of pride in the role that he played.

Later on in the spring of the year following the Montana incident, Tommy Lee informed Will that *The Mudpuppies* were scheduled to perform at a venue up on Long Island. Will assured him that he would attend.

At the concert, before playing their last number, "Lesbian Girl", Tommy Lee held the mike in his hand and walked to the edge of the stage. There, he pointed to Will in the audience and announced, "We got a very special guest with us in the audience tonight, y'all. We'd like for him to join us up on the stage." As Will got out of his seat, very much surprised and delighted, Tommy Lee continued. "I'd like to introduce y'all to the gentleman who wrote the lyrics to the song you're goin' to hear next. Why don't y'all give him a warm welcome... the man who wrote *Lesbian Girl* hisself...Mister Wiiiiiilll Kraft!*"

OK, the wild applause wasn't all that wild, and it didn't literally last *fifteen minutes,* but you get the idea...

Not surprisingly, the *Mudpuppies* were a big draw at Lesbian music festivals and gay pride events. Their smash hit, "Lesbian Girl", is the song that every crowd eagerly awaits. They now do an epic jam version that they first introduced at a festival up in the Catskills that has the crowd waltzin' and a-rockin' for over a half hour!

Will's personal fantasy is that someday the band will call him up to the stage again, and when he's up there, the young lady who inspired the song, the one back at the *Mons Venus,* will be in the crowd. They'll make eye-contact, and she'll give him that shy little wave. He'll then call on her to join him up on the stage and introduce her, maybe even tell the story of that evening under the Spanish Moss back in southern Georgia. Imagine her surprise. Imagine the tragedy if she were to live out her entire life never knowing that she was the inspiration for that song.

By the way, you may also recall that Will was wearing his favorite shirt that night in Georgia, the com-fort-a-bly-love-ly one. *The Mysterious Mudpuppies* now also do a cover of Donovan's "shirt song". Not that you would actually recognize it. This new version has a kind of a Lynard Skynyrd Southern Rock Quality and goes on for over twenty minutes during live performances. Adding that song to the band's set list was also something that Will suggested.. But he takes no credit. He had already gotten his fifteen minutes of fame.

CHAPTER 34

AND THE ROAD GOES ON FOREVER .

———∿———

And what about Annie and Will, as a couple, that is? They had promised to stay in touch, and that they did, by telephone, every evening, until the kidnapping incident.

After emerging from the wilderness and while in the protective custody of the FBI, Will finally found time to call again. Though they spoke for over an hour, Will said nothing about being in protective custody. Neither did he mention anything about his encounter with The Front. He just didn't think it would have been a good idea to have a phone conversation that began with: "Annie, please sit down. I am going to share with you a harrowing tale that would be best heard in a seated position, with a mind open to the improbable." Some things should not be shared by telephone.

Instead, he chose to tell Annie about the wonderful the time spent in The Bob filled with vivid descriptions of the natural beauty and the wildlife. All in all it had been very *eventful,* he told her. Some of those events, in fact, might strain believability. So much so, he thought, that he decided it might be best to put everything in writing. He would send her an essay entitled "What I did on my Summer Vacation", his take on the tried and true writing project that generations of American school children are assigned upon returning to school in the fall. "I put my story in a brown Manila envelope and you should get it within a day or two. By that time, I should be back on Long Island."

When the envelope arrived a few days later, Annie immediately took it up to her bedroom to read in privacy. She had no idea what to make of it. It was truly a bizarre tale, surreal actually, of abduction, captivity and escape involving apocalyptic characters and a super-hero Hutterite. *All right,* she thought to herself, *if you want to have some fun with me, I'll play right along.*

Annie took out a red pen and started. First she corrected some spelling and grammatical errors. She cut Will some slack as far as punctuation was concerned. Commas especially. There no longer seems to be a right and wrong with them, anyway. Annie suggested that the story would flow better with some changes in syntax. She filled the margin with anecdotal remarks, and clearly did her best to keep things positive.

When it came time for a grade, she gave Will a B+ with an explanation— written in red of course— "…although you submitted a cleverly written piece of fiction, it fell short on verisimilitude (the appearance of reality). Fiction is always more effective within the context of **believability**. She went on to point out the specific parts that might appeal only to gullible readers. "Come on, Will! A 'Flying' Hoot?"

Like any good teacher, she offered encouragement and the opportunity for extra-help. "I would be willing to offer private tutoring services to help you achieve your potential, if you could be willing to avail yourself of my services," she added, somewhat naughtily.

Along with the essay, Will had also placed an invitation in the envelope: an offer to spend a long weekend together in Asheville, North Carolina, about halfway between Austin and New York. "We've got some catching-up to do," he wrote. "Say yes, and I'll book flights ASAP!"

During that evening's phone conversation, Annie sounded more cheerful than usual. "I got your essay," she said immediately. "But first, as far as Asheville goes…book those flights immediately!"

"So back to the essay," Annie continued. It was soon clear from her critique that she honestly thought Will had written a little playful fiction piece. Maybe to try and impress her with his creativity.

Imagine the difficulty Will had trying to convince Annie that it was not a "fiction piece", but a real-life-true story! Because parts of the story had to be explained several times, it was almost two hours before he was finished.

"You know, Annie," he conceded, "If someone had told this story to me, I'm not so sure I would have believed it myself. Why don't we wait till we're in Asheville, and then I can tell you the whole thing in person."

Annie agreed that would be a good idea.

Will and Annie continued their once a day (…and often more) phone conversations. When the long weekend in Asheville came… and it couldn't have come soon enough…it was an unqualified success. I guess you could say that their romance truly blossomed during those four days in the Great Smoky Mountains.

They would continue the pattern of meeting at least once a month in Austin, on Long Island or places in between, like Savannah and Charleston. Then something happened that put an end to the *long-distance* part of their relationship.

During the spring of the following year, Annie started a phone conversation with some exciting news. Her publishing company needed a person with her qualifications to fill a vacancy in the downtown Manhattan office. There would be a substantial increase in pay based on cost of living. In other words, a promotion. Would she be interested?

"What are you going to tell them?" Asked Will, with a bit of hesitation.

"I haven't gotten back to them. I told them I need time to think it over. Actually, the truth is I'd like to take the position, but first I wanted to hear how you felt about it, Will."

Will responded with another question. "Is a girl from Austin ready for The Big Apple?"

"The real question, Will? The real question here, is a boy from Long Island ready for a girl from Austin, Texas?"

"Annie, I'm going out on a limb here, but dare I be so bold as to assume that you're asking to domicile with me…please don't tell me that I must have misunderstood!"

"No," replied Annie, "you understood perfectly well. And that's what I need from you, Will… not just a 'yes', but an unequivocal '**yes!**"

On the very first day of Will's summer vacation, he boarded a one-way flight to Austin. Annie had already hitched a trailer loaded with her prized possessions on to the back of Beulah the Buick. A few days later with Walter in the backseat and Willie Nelson on the stereo, they were on their way to Long Island.

CHAPTER 35

REUNION AFTER REUNION

———— ⌇ ————

Annie and Will had been living together for almost a year when they received an invitation from Will's German friends, Martin and Iris. Since serving as Will's accomplices in the Little Big Horn caper, they had formed a bond of sorts.

"Visit us in Germany, why don't you?" Martin wrote. "We will arrange for you to see many historical sites, and at the moment your dollar is very strong!"

"Why not?" encouraged Annie. "It's been five years since I was last in Europe. Besides, I've heard so much about this couple."

A few months later they arrived at Stuttgart Airport. Martin and Iris greeted them with an enormous "Wilkommen in Deutschland" banner. It was 10AM German time (4 AM in NY), but jet-lagged as they may have been, they soon found themselves sitting in a filled-to-capacity soccer stadium, drinking beer and rooting for the home team.

Although their circadian rhythm had yet to return to normal, the following day they were visiting the Mercedes-Benz Museum where Will paid special attention to the Gelandeswagen, the G-Wagen. The spectacle of the G-Wagen immediately conjured up a flashback of Tillman Smith. Will couldn't help wonder how The Front leader was spending his time in prison.

Over an dinner of roast beef with onions and Spaetzle (*ausgezeichnet!*) that evening, lovingly prepared by their hosts (and with the Dinkelacker flowing), Martin and Iris heard the nightmarish tale of the kidnapping for the first time. They sat and listened with jaws dropped.

"And we thought we had such a grand adventure at Little Big Horn!" Iris exclaimed. "Even Karl May could not tell such a great story!"

Just as the cuckoo clock in the dining room chimed midnight, Will had just been wrapping up his story. Martin wisely suggested, "Perhaps we should all get to bed. We will be needing an early start tomorrow."

They had been in Germany for less than two days. The Wetzels had been eager for their guests to partake in the regional cuisine, and did not miss an opportunity. Under the soft comforter, Annie cuddled up to Will. "I have a question," she whispered. "When we get back to the states, what should we enroll in first, Weight Watchers or Alcoholics Annonymous?"

The following day, their European vacation began in earnest. The road trip would many sites of historical significance. Places that Will's Global History students had learned about, but even Will himself had never seen firsthand: castles, battlefields and Gothic cathedrals aplenty. Although Martin and Iris had curated the experience with Will the historian in mind, they hardly neglected offerings such as concerts, and of course, culinary experiences and wine tastings.

The final destination together was Munich. Time was set aside for a somber visit to the former Dachau concentration camp. As they walked through the grounds, Will wondered how something so horrific could have happened. That dark stain on Germany's past belied the cheerful and convivial people they had experienced throughout their stay, the famous *Gemutlichkeit* of the German people. During their visit to Dachau, Will's thoughts turned to the members of The Front back in Montana. Might they benefit from a visit to such a concentration camp, perhaps experience a change of heart? Would time spent here help them recognize what can happen when their kind of racial and religious bigotry takes root? Or would they simply dismiss the whole thing as a hoax? Or even worse, conclude that what had happened here was just.

Over dinner that evening, the Wetzels offered an apology. It had become obvious to them that Dachau had caused Will and Annie considerable distress.

Iris attempted to explain. "Our generation experiences so much *Schuld*—guilt-- over what our parents did during the time of Hitler. We always think it is necessary to show others our shame. Of course, we Germans have come up with a word for it, *Vergangenheitsbewaltigung* — "coping with the past"— not the longest word in the German vocabulary by the way.

Annie took the initiative and responded. "No apology necessary. Surely the experience was upsetting, and we weren't quite prepared for our... strong reaction. But it was important for us to see, and to feel this."

"And as a history teacher," Will added, "it is especially important to actually visit those places about which I teach my students."

Iris and Martin wished to shift the mood the following day. This would, after all, be their final full day in Germany. They decided that a relaxing stroll through Munich's famous English Garden in the city's center would be perfect.

At first, the park reminded Will of Manhattan's Central Park, but the nude bathing beach along the bank of the Eisbach River served as a reminder that they were in Bavaria. The evening was spent eating, drinking and dancing in the park's famous *Biergarten* where a band was performing in a Chinese Pagoda. That experience ended any further comparisons to Central Park!

Before long, they were all feeling a bit tipsy. Soon enough, under the capable tutelage of the Wetzels, Will and Annie were waltzing their way through the warm Bavarian evening.

With intervals of tears, but mostly laughter, Martin recalled with great delight the act of sedition at Little Big Horn. "We Germans are such ridiculous rule-followers," he said self-deprecatingly. "It gave us great pleasure to help Will do something illegal!"

Then Martin raised his beer mug, "Cheers to the rule- breakers!"

Many more toasts followed, both in English and German. To new friendships (*neue Freundschaften)!* To travel and expanding horizons *(erweiterte Horizonte)!* To broadening vistas *(erweiterte Ausblicke)!* All of which they were living, after all!

Next morning, the bittersweet inevitability of parting ways arrived. The couples made a pact to see each other again, on one side of the Atlantic or the other.

"But I don't think it will be necessary for us to become 'blood brothers' like Old Shatterhand and Winnetou," Martin laughed, once again hearkening back to Karl May's writings. The farewell was especially tearful for Annie and Iris, who had truly bonded during their time spent together.

After the Wetzels departed, Annie and Will took the trolley to an auto rental facility to pick up a BMW that they would drive to their next destination, Innsbruck, Austria.

As bonding experiences go, sharing the cockpit of a Ford pickup with someone while hurtling forty six feet across a river is hard to beat. Then again, in the case of Will and Hal Miller, they seemed to have hit it off quite well right from the get-go with their shared interest in European history. So maybe that river-leaping episode wasn't really necessary to forge this most unlikely friendship between the confirmed agnostic and the pious Hutterite.

Anyhow, a while back when Will had written Hal that he and Annie were planning to visit some folks in Germany and spend a few days in Munich, Hal did some quick calculations.

"Do you know that by car, Innsbruck, Austria is less than two hours from Munich?" Hal informed them. "Why not pay a visit? After all, Innsbruck is the city where the martyrdom of Jacob Hutter took place, kind of a birthplace for us Hutterites. While you're there, maybe you could do a little research on our founding father."

As an afterthought, Hal wrote, "I wish I could go with you and speed a hundred and forty miles an hour on the Autobahn!"

That's how Innsbruck was added to the itinerary. How could Will deny Hal his request? They even made arrangements to meet with a local historian, a vivacious young lady named Sybylla.

In Austria, Will and Annie spent two very productive days gathering information on all things Hutterite. They would subsequently share their newfound knowledge with Hal. Some of that information was new even to Hal, if you can believe that. When Will returned to The States he made sure to add some of that material to his American History curriculum. It fit nicely into the religious freedom unit.

In addition to the Wetzels and Hal Miller, Will also stayed in touch with Henry "Hawk" Hawksbill. The burying of the artifacts at Little Big Horn had indeed restored peace to Hawk's troubled soul, and for that he would remain forever grateful to Will. Still, it came as quite a surprise when Will and Annie received an invitation to join Hawk on a road trip in his brand new RV.

The itinerary would include a number of Native-American Pow-Wows and many historical sites throughout the West. "I'm retired now," explained Hawk, "and this is something the Missus and I always wanted to do. I can't think of anyone better to share the adventure with than you and Annie... and be sure to bring your boys!" They barely got over the jet-lag of the European vacation, and were now headed west.

As for taking the boys along, Will expected resistance from his ex-wife, but she didn't require much persuasion. "Just think of the educational value this experience will have for the boys. They'll be entering fifth and seventh grade, perfect ages to experience history first hand," was his rationale.

So she did allow them to go along, but insisted that it be five days and five days only, simply because Katie had always been a bit of a control freak, or at least that's how Will saw it. Of course, Annie would be going along as well. This delighted the boys. She was a real "softy" who could never say no to them, not ever.

Those five days spent with Hawk and his wife turned out to be memorable indeed. They even spent a full day at Little Big Horn. For the boys, it was especially thrilling to be standing on the actual ground where Custer had fought his last battle. They had learned so much about him in school. An especially poignant moment took place when Will requested some time alone with Hawk. Will led his friend to the exact location where he had buried the artifacts. There, the two men stood solemnly together for a few minutes, not saying a word. At one point, Will discreetly turned to look at his friend. Hawk was facing upward to the sky, eyes closed, a tear rolling down the side of his face.

They went as far as Billings with Hawk and his wife in the RV. There they had reserved a rental car to drive further west, and pay a visit to Hal Miller at the Hutterite colony. Hal was disappointed when he found out that Will and his family would only be staying overnight. "You've come all this way," he argued. "Why not stay with us a few extra days?"

Will said to Hal that it may not be that easy, he would have to clear it with his ex-wife. Katie was indeed not happy about the breach of agreement.

"You said five days!" she reminded him. Then she completely lost it and accused Will of kidnapping the children to *join a cult.* Those were her actual words.

Will was finally able to convince her, after a two hour telephone conversation that is. He kept hammering home the cultural value of the experience. Exasperated, Will put Hal Miller, *the Flying Hoot* himself on the phone. In his kindly voice, Hal asked Katie, "When will two boys from the Long Island suburbs ever again get a chance to help out with farm animals?" Within a few minutes, he had brokered an agreement that allowed Eric and Paul to spend some extra days helping out on a genuine Hutterite colony. Will probably should have put Hal on the phone sooner.

"I think I'm pregnant, Will." Those words came out of Annie's mouth a few weeks after they had returned back to Long Island.

"What??!!"

"You heard me right. I think we're going to be parents. And I did the math…"

"You did the math? What math are we talking about here, Annie?"

"Remember the day back in Austria when we packed a picnic basket and a bottle of *Gruner Veltliner* and drove off into the mountains? On the return, we pulled off into a scenic overlook with a great view of Innsbruck. As we we were parked, I popped a Strauss Waltz into the CD player."

"Yes. If I recall, it was 'The Blue Danube'."

"Wrong," Annie corrected. "It was 'Tales from the Vienna Woods'."

"Right.…right! That's the one. You proposed making love right then and there, so we could have some tales of our own from the Vienna Woods. I reminded you that we were in Innsbruck, not Vienna, and you said why quibble over details. We were laughing so hard that you could hardly pull my pants down…"

"But I managed," said Annie with a wink.

"You certainly did, my love. The next thing I knew, you were getting real naughty and pretty much had your way with me."

"I'd like to think that we were two consenting adults!"

"That we were!"

"So I did the math," Annie continued. Conception must have taken place in the BMW while listening to Strauss."

"Conception in a motor vehicle! Imagine that, it's like *déjà vu* all over again!"

"Exactly," laughed Annie.

The Wedding took place five months later.

Will had asked his long-time friend Bob Tuxson to be Best Man. Knowing that everyone loves a good "How did you two meet?" story, he prepared the hilarious tale of how hitchhiker Will got picked up by Annie (and Walter) in her old Buick station wagon, with embellishments, as if the story needed them. He even shared the story of that romantic evening in the rented BMW in Austria.

The Best Man speech caught Will and Annie by surprise.

"Is nothing 'sacred' anymore?" Annie whispered in Will's ear.

"I guess not," replied Will.

Up until that point, no one except a few of the couple's besties were familiar with the story of how they met, and certainly *not* the parents! So the cat was let out of the bag, about that and a few other things. All the guests went home with something to talk about. For a long time to come.

It was a colorful assemblage indeed. The guest list included Hal Miller, who came all the way from Montana with his wife, resplendent in Hutterite finery. Hawk and the Missus were there as well, and they wowed the crowd in their stunning Cherokee/Choctaw regalia. Martin Wetzel stood out in his Lederhosen and Iris attracted considerable attention in a *cleavaredge*-revealing *Dirndl*. Mathias Keller, the FBI agent, was well-dressed, but in an incognito sort of way. Homage was paid most favorably to the State of Texas by Annie's dad and mom with their bodacious vintage western shirts. Not to be outdone, Will's dad sported the latest in the Serpentino collection, which had recently expanded into a men's line. Mom, of course, sported the now famous…in Florida, at least…Serpentino Stilettos, but they came off quickly once the dancing began.

And did they ever dance! It was almost impossible to get folks off that dance floor! The band even struck up a country-rock interpretation of a Strauss Waltz, "Tales from Vienna Woods", something you don't hear much at weddings anymore. They did a bunch of other quirky numbers as well, that delighted the guests to no end. In fact, as the evening concluded and well after the music ended, the guests could not stop talking about the incredible band. It was some group that came up all the way from Georgia. They went by the name of "Tommy Lee Clarke and the Mysterious Mudpuppies."

-THE END-

ABOUT THE AUTHOR

After retiring from his teaching career , Erwin "Erv" Krause finally found the time needed to devote to his love of writing. His first book, "Escape from the USA", published in 2017, describes a real-life motorcycle misadventure undertaken by Krause and his buddy during the tumultuous 1960s. His latest work, "Escape from The Front", is his first fiction piece. Any similarity in titles completely intentional.

Krause lives in Oakdale, Long Island and Manhattan's Upper East Side with his long-time partner and muse, Lois Hoffman. Before you try to just drop in on them, call first. There's a good chance that their shared love of adventure travel will find them in some far-flung corner of the globe or maybe just hiking in the nearby Catskill Mountains.